FLASH FICTION

ALSO EDITED BY JAMES THOMAS

The Best of the West, 1–4 (with Denise Thomas)
Sudden Fiction International (with Robert Shapard)
Sudden Fiction (with Robert Shapard)

ALSO BY JAMES THOMAS

Pictures, Moving (Stories)

FLASH FICTION

VERY SHORT STORIES

Edited by
James Thomas, Denise Thomas,
and Tom Hazuka

W. W. NORTON & COMPANY

New York   London

Special thanks to the Department of English and the College of Liberal
Arts at Wright State University for their generous support; to the many
students at Wright State who helped in the selection of these stories; and
to Chris Merrill, Alan Cheuse, and Nat Sobel for their time and advice.

The acknowledgments on page 217 are an extension of the copyright page.

Printed in the United States of America
First Edition
The text of this book is composed in Weiss with the
display set in Serif Gothic Bold
Composition by PennSet, Inc.
Manufacturing by Courier Companies, Inc.
Book design by Charlotte Staub

Library of Congress Cataloging-in-Publication Data

Flash fiction : very short stories / edited by James Thomas,
   Denise Thomas, and Tom Hazuka
   p. cm.
   1. Short stories, American   I. Thomas, James
   II. Thomas, Denise   III. Hazuka, Tom
   PS648.S5F58   1992
   813'.0108—dc20   91-42347

ISBN 0-393-03361-9 (cl)
ISBN 0-393-30883-9 (pa)

W.W. Norton & Company, Inc.
500 Fifth Avenue
New York, N.Y. 10110
W.W. Norton & Company Ltd.
10 Coptic Street
London WC1A 1PU

1 2 3 4 5 6 7 8 9 0

C.\

For Carol Houck Smith,
a reader's reader, an editor's editor,
and a great good friend to writers.

CONTENTS

CONTENTS

INTRODUCTION

How short can a story be and still truly be a story? This book attempts to provide a collective response to that question, although any answer, surely, will remain subjective. How short is *very?* Hemingway's wonderful (and classic) "A Very Short Story" is about 750 words, and none of the stories here is much longer than that. Nor do any of the stories included in this anthology run less than 250 words, the diminutive *limit* that Jerome Stern has put to his "World's Best Short-Short Story" competition, the winners of which appear each fall in *Sundog: The Southeast Review.*

Why *Flash Fiction* as opposed to *Sudden Fiction*, which we have featured in two previous books? Answer: We *did* want to make a distinction between the two types of stories. The stories here are shorter (in terms of "limit") by a full thousand words than the stories in those books, and quantitatively there is a big difference between 1,750 words and 750 words. In terms of quality, however, we would maintain that the stories here are as fully dimensional and wholly complete as the *Sudden* stories. Like all fiction that matters, their success depends not on their length but on their depth, their clarity of vision, their human significance—the extent to which the reader is able to recognize in them the real stuff of real life.

But less *can* sometimes be more, we think: the meaningful glance more consequential than the long (but less intense, less informed) look or stare. These stories are not tricks, or trills on a flute; rather they are very short stage presentations or musical pieces that play to the full range of human sensibilities—some evoke mood while others provoke the intellect, some introduce us to people we're interested to meet, while others tell us of unusual but understandable phenomena in this world, and some of them do several or all of these things, the things good fiction of any length does.

One of our original ideas for the book was to present stories that could be read without turning a page, assuming that there might be some difference in the way we read stories when we can actually *see* beginning and end at the same time. So, envisioning a story on a two-page spread, 750 words seemed about tops for conventional, readable typography. Enthusiastically, we began searching for such stories, and called them "flash" fictions because there would be no enforced pause in the reader's concentration, no break in the field of vision. They would be apprehended "all at once."

Over a period of three years we found them, thousands of them, hundreds of which we asked our literary friends and my writing students at Wright State University to read. We asked them to read them and rate them (on a score of one to ten), stirred in our own "scores," and when it came time we delivered these seventy-two stories to the publisher, saying, "remember, one story to a page (or a two-page spread), just a little book of little stories." What we hadn't anticipated was the physical monotony of such a book *design*, story page after story page, and what we hadn't accounted for was the obvious, if illusory, notion that as readers we expect and *like* to turn pages. Turning pages, it would seem, is part of what fiction is about, part of the passing of the story.

We therefore adjusted our vision (but kept the title) and allowed the stories to begin and to end, to proceed through the book, in a more natural and conventional way. Now what we read before we turn the page has the effect of allowing the story to ascend, to gain altitude, you might say, before seeing and therefore anticipating the landing strip.

The minimal and rapid trajectory is of course much of the appeal (and challenge) of these stories—but it is interesting to note that that public taste for brevity in fiction has fluctuated over the years. Fifty years ago very short stories could be found in such magazines as *Liberty*, but fifteen years ago it was most unusual to come across a story of under five pages in the respected magazines and literary journals of this country. It's hard to know whether writers fifteen years ago weren't writing these stories or editors simply weren't accepting them for publication, but I'm inclined to think (as both an editor and a writer at that time) that editors were declining to publish very short fictions, considering them "slight," if not whimsical. Then writers like Raymond Carver and Joyce Carol Oates started producing them, literary magazines like *The North American Review* started printing them, and by the end of the eighties the form (which at two thousand words we've called "sudden fiction") had a fervent following and was being widely published. Now, *very* short pieces, under a thousand words, have been appearing with greater frequency, and we can only wonder, as we introduce you to the stories in this volume—welcome, welcome, welcome, enjoy, enjoy, enjoy—whether "flash fiction" will be an avid endeavor of the present literary generation.

It is a distinct pleasure to wonder about this with you, students of fiction all of us, and to present to you these stories along with the question, "How short can a story be and . . . ?"

—James Thomas

FLASH FICTION

BRILLIANT
SILENCE

Two Alaskan Kodiak bears joined a small circus where the pair appeared in a nightly parade pulling a covered wagon. The two were taught to somersault, to spin, to stand on their heads, and to dance on their hind legs, paw in paw, stepping in unison. Under a spotlight the dancing bears, a male and a female, soon became favorites of the crowd. The circus went south on a west coast tour through Canada to California and on down into Mexico, through Panama into South America, down the Andes the length of Chile to those southernmost isles of Tierra del Fuego.

There a jaguar jumped the juggler, and afterwards, mortally mauled the animal trainer; and the shocked showpeople disbanded in dismay and horror. In the confusion the bears went their own way. Without a master, they wandered off by themselves into the wilderness on those densely wooded, wildly windy, subantarctic islands. Utterly away from people, on an out-of-the-way uninhabited island, and in a climate they found ideal, the bears mated, thrived, multiplied, and after a number of generations populated the entire island. Indeed, after some years, descendants of the two moved out onto half a dozen adjacent islands; and seventy years later, when scientists finally found and enthusiastically studied the bears, it was discovered that all of them, to a bear, were performing splendid circus tricks.

On nights when the sky is bright and the moon is full, they gather to dance. They gather the cubs and the juveniles in a circle around them. They gather together out of the wind at the center of a sparkling, circular crater left by a meteorite which had fallen in a bed of chalk. Its glassy walls are chalk white, its flat floor is covered with white gravel, and it is well-drained, and dry. No vegetation grows within. When the moon rises above it, the light reflecting off the walls fills the crater with a pool of moonlight, so that it is twice as bright on the crater floor as anywhere else in that vicinity. Scientists speculate that originally the full moon had reminded the two bears of the circus spotlight, and for that reason they danced. Yet, it might be asked, what music do the descendants dance to?

Paw in paw, stepping in unison . . . what music can they possibly hear inside their heads as they dance under the full moon and the Aurora Australis, as they dance in brilliant silence?

PUMPKINS

There is a terrible accident. A truck full of Halloween pumpkins is speeding around a curve and fails to see another car unwisely making a U-turn. In the car is a young woman, married, the mother of three, who, when the vehicles collide, is killed.

Actually, she is beheaded, her body thrown from the car and decapitated with such force that the head sails through the air and lands in a pile of pumpkins spilled out onto the road.

Her husband is spared this detail until the next day, when it appears in a front page story in the local paper.

This newspaper is bought by a woman about to leave home on a trip. The tragedy so unhinges her that she rushes off the train and calls her husband at work. When she mentions the pumpkin-truck accident, he says, Pumpkin-truck accident? precisely like their five-year-old son saying, Bubble gum on the couch?

The woman begins to tremble, realizing now what she should have realized (and because she is in therapy, she thinks, she *did* realize, no wonder she was upset!). The accident occurred more or less exactly in front of the house of a woman with whom her husband had a love affair but has promised he has stopped seeing.

She senses that her husband knows about this accident—and not from reading the newspaper. That is why he sounds guilty. Perhaps he was with his lover when it happened, perhaps this woman called him for comfort, just as she is calling him now. As she confronts him with this, her husband keeps interrupting to answer questions at his office.

The next morning the woman sees her therapist on an emergency basis. She tells him the whole story, from buying the paper and reading about the pumpkin-truck to calling her husband to her husband moving out again last night.

The therapist says he is sorry; he cannot talk about this. He tells her that, coincidentally, one of his patients is the husband of the woman killed by the pumpkin-truck. It is, after all, a small town. The therapist says he has been dealing with this tragedy for two days—on a *real* crisis basis, a *real* emergency basis—and frankly he cannot stand to hear it treated as another subplot in this woman's continuing romantic imbroglio.

The woman bursts into tears. The therapist apologizes for his unprofessional behavior; he says the whole thing has unnerved him in ways even he doesn't understand.

That night the therapist tells his wife about this. For ethical reasons he leaves out the names. Still, he repeats what the woman told him and what he said and what happened.

Except that this time, instead of saying "pumpkins," he says "Christmas trees."

"Christmas trees?" says his wife.

"Did I say Christmas trees?" he says. "How funny. I meant pumpkins." Naturally he realizes that this slip of the tongue is a clue to why this incident so disturbs him.

Later, in bed, he considers his mistake. And before long it comes to him. Because for once the truth is not submerged, but bobs on the surface, like a buoy, tied to a time he often revisits in looking back on his life.

At five he suffered a case of mumps which turned into something more serious. He remembers running to his parents' room, his cheeks swinging like sacks of flesh from his face. He remembers falling. After that he was sick for months—from autumn through early winter. The symbolism is so obvious: pumpkin time when he became ill, Christmas when he recovered.

Now his wife gets into bed, but he doesn't notice. For he is feeling, as never before, how much of his life has passed: all the years that separate him from that swollen-faced boy. He thinks how sweet that period was, the rhythm of those days, sleep, radio, chilled canned pears, the kingdom of the blanket, the kingdom of ice outside it.

For an instant he nearly recaptures that haze of safety, confusion and boredom, when he fell asleep looking at pumpkins and awoke seeing a Christmas tree, when nothing scared him, not even time, it was all being taken care of. Then it recedes like the plots of dreams he wakes up already forgetting.

It is like the experience of speeding along a highway, and some broken sign or ruined cafe will suddenly recall his past, but before he can tell his wife, they have already driven by. He knows that if he turns and goes back, what caught his eye will have vanished—though perhaps he may catch a glimpse of it, fleeing from him down the road.

Richard Shelton

THE STONES

I love to go out on summer nights and watch the stones grow. I think they grow better here in the desert, where it is warm and dry, than almost anywhere else. Or perhaps it is only that the young ones are more active here.

Young stones tend to move about more than their elders consider good for them. Most young stones have a secret desire which their parents had before them but have forgotten ages ago. And because this desire involves water, it is never mentioned. The older stones disapprove of water and say, "Water is a gadfly who never stays in one place long enough to learn anything." But the young stones try to work themselves into a position, slowly and without their elders noticing it, in which a sizable stream of water during a summer storm might catch them broadside and unknowing, so to speak, and push them along over a slope or down an arroyo. In spite of the danger this involves, they want to travel and see something of the world and settle in a new place, far from home, where they can raise their own dynasties away from the domination of their parents.

And although family ties are very strong among stones, many of the more daring young ones have succeeded; and they carry scars to prove to their children that they once went on a journey, helter-skelter and high water, and traveled perhaps fifteen feet, an incredible distance. As they grow older, they cease to brag about such clandestine adventures.

It is true that old stones get to be very conservative. They consider all movement either dangerous or downright sinful. They remain comfortable where they are and often get fat. Fatness, as a matter of fact, is a mark of distinction.

And on summer nights, after the young stones are asleep, the elders turn to a serious and frightening subject—the moon, which is always spoken of in whispers. "See how it glows and whips across the sky, always changing its shape," one says. And another says, "Feel how it pulls at us, urging us to follow." And a third whispers, "It is a stone gone mad."

Joanna H. Woś

THE ONE
SITTING THERE

I threw away the meat. The dollar ninety-eight a pound ground beef, the boneless chicken, the spareribs, the hamsteak. I threw the soggy vegetables into the trashcan: the carrots, broccoli, peas, the Brussels sprouts. I poured the milk down the drain of the stainless steel sink. The cheddar cheese I ground up in the disposal. The ice cream, now liquid, followed. All the groceries in the refrigerator had to be thrown away. The voice on the radio hinted of germs thriving on the food after the hours without power. Throwing the food away was rational and rea-sonable.

In our house, growing up, you were never allowed to throw food away. There was a reason. My mother saved peelings and spoiled things to put on the compost heap. That would go back into the garden to grow more vegetables. You could leave meat or potatoes to be used again in soup. But you were never allowed to throw food away.

I threw the bread away. The bread had gotten wet. I once saw my father pick up a piece of Wonder Bread he had dropped on the ground. He brushed his hand over the slice to remove the dirt and then kissed the bread. Even at six I knew why he did that. My sister was the reason. I was born after the war. She lived in a time before. I do not know much about her. My mother never talked about her. There are no pictures. The only time my father talked about her was when he described how she clutched the bread so tightly in her baby fist that the bread squeezed out between her fingers. She sucked at the bread that way.

So I threw the bread away last. I threw the bread away for all the times I sat crying over a bowl of cabbage soup my father said I had to eat. Because eating would not bring her back. Because I would still be the one sitting there. Now I had the bread. I had gotten it. I had bought it. I had put it in the refrigerator. I had earned it. It was mine to throw away.

So I threw the bread away for my sister. I threw the bread away and brought her back. She was twenty-one and had just come home from Christmas shopping. She had bought me a doll. She put the package on my dining room table and hung her coat smelling of perfume and the late fall air on the back of one of the chairs. I welcomed her as an honored guest. As if she were a Polish bride returning to her home, I greeted her with a plate of bread and salt. The bread, for prosperity, was wrapped in a white linen cloth. The salt, for tears, was in a small blue bowl. We sat down together and shared a piece of bread.

In a kitchen, where such an act was an ordinary thing, I threw away the bread. Because I could.

CROSSING
SPIDER CREEK

Here is a seriously injured man on a frightened horse.
They are high in the Rocky Mountains at the junction of the
Roosevelt Trail and Spider Creek. Tom has tried to coax the horse
into the freezing water twice before. Both times the horse started
to cross then lost its nerve, swung around violently, and lunged
back up the bank. The pivot and surge of power had been nearly
too much for Tom. Both times he almost lost his grip on the
saddlehorn and fell into the boulders of the creek bank. Both
times, when it seemed his hold would fail, he had thought of his

wife, Carol. He will try the crossing once more. It will take all the strength he has left.

This is not the Old West. It is nineteen eighty-seven, autumn, a nice day near the beginning of elk season. Two days ago Tom had led the horse, his camp packed in panniers hung over the saddle, up this same trail. He had some trouble getting the horse to cross the creek but it hadn't been bad. This was a colt, Carol's colt and well broke to lead. It had come across without much fuss. But that was before the nice weather had swelled Spider Creek with runoff, and of course the colt had not had the smell of blood in his nostrils.

Tom's injury is a compound fracture of the right femur. He has wrapped it tightly with an extra cotton shirt but he cannot stop the bleeding. The blood covers the right shoulder of the horse, the rifle scabbard, and the saddle from the seat to the stirrup. Tom knows that it is the loss of blood that is making him so weak. He wonders if that is why his thoughts keep wandering from what he is trying to do here, with the horse, to Carol. She has never understood his desire to be alone. From time to time, over the years, she has complained that he cares less for her than for solitude. He has always known that is not true. But still it seems vaguely funny to him that now she is all he wants to think about. He wishes she could know that, hopes he will have a chance to tell her.

Perhaps it is being on this particular horse, he thinks, the one Carol likes better than any of the others. Maybe Carol has spent enough time with this horse to have become part of it.

The horse moves nervously under him as he reins it around to face the water again. Tom wishes there were a way to ease the animal through this. But there is not, and there is clearly little time. There is just this one last chance.

They begin to move slowly down the bank again. It will be all or nothing. If the horse makes it across Spider Creek they will simply ride down the trail, be at a campground in twenty minutes. There are other hunters there. They will get him to a hospital. If the horse refuses and spins in fear, Tom will fall. The horse will clamber up the bank and stand aloof, quaking with terror and forever out of reach. Tom sees himself bleeding to death, alone, by the cascading icy water.

As the horse stretches out its nose to sniff at the water, Tom thinks that there might be time, if he falls, to grab at the rifle and drag it from the scabbard as he goes down. He clucks to the horse and it moves forward. Though he would hate to, it might be possible to shoot the horse from where he would fall. With luck he would have the strength to crawl to it and hold its warm head for a few moments before they died. It would be best for Carol if they were found like that.

Here is a seriously injured man on a frightened horse. They are standing at the edge of Spider Creek, the horse's trembling front feet in the water and the man's spurs held an inch from the horse's flanks.

Allen Woodman

THE LAMPSHADE VENDOR

It was typical. The door was open. It was summer. The TV was on.

A white-haired man dressed in a black and frayed tuxedo came to the door selling lampshades. He was a dignified man transformed by the loss of his hands. He picked up a shade with one of his metal claws. "Sell you a new lampshade?"

I didn't like the shade. I had never even given much thought to the lampshades I already had. I wondered how he lost his hands. I tried to make conversation. "A man knocked on the door yesterday selling mops and brooms. Do you know him?"

He put the lampshade back on his cart. "No relation. I sell shades. You want one?"

I've always loved human activities that are on the way out. I asked him how long he had sold lampshades.

"Fifteen years ago, I had a sideshow at all the big fairs, a flea circus. But I was hit hard by hygiene and taste."

"I saw a flea circus once, but no one believes me," I said. "I keep it to myself. But I'd swear I remember a tiny flea wedding and a flea riding on a bicycle."

"I had a little table for the stage, and I would only allow a few chairs for the audience. I had a ballet sequence, a tightrope walk, and a wagon train race. The secret was all in the human flea. They are the only ones with the necessary power to tug and push with their back legs. My fleas were incredible. What stamina. They could perform hundreds of shows a day, and continue for weeks. And at the end of my show, I would roll back my sleeve and invite the performers to dine." The man raised his chrome hooks in the air.

"I read that in Mexico, the Church supported flea art," I said. "Nuns made and sold miniature models of the Stations of the Cross fashioned out of flea corpses and scrap materials. The fleas kept them from having to carve human figures."

"I had a flea," he said in a quiet voice. "I kept it as a pet. It was the only one I let suck the palm of my hand. I fastened it to a chain of gold no longer than your finger. I attached a perfectly shaped coach of gold to the chain for the flea to pull."

I thought I'd seen everything. But the way he talked about this pet flea and the perfect gold coach got me to thinking. "Yes," I said, my voice rising, "do you think you could tell me about it again?"

He stared at me. "No," he said, cautiously. "It's hard on me to remember."

I tried to think of a proper response. "I understand," I said, finally.

The man rubbed one of his metal claws against the skin under his chin. "Wait a minute," he said. "Get me something to write with."

He picked up one of the plain white lampshades. I placed a pen in his left claw. It was a felt tip that I had forgotten to return to the clerk when I wrote a check at the A&P.

He drew the whole flea circus on the shade, the wedding, the tightrope walker, and a flea ballet. He drew scenes we hadn't even talked about. Finally he drew what I knew had to be the flea on the golden chain, for it rested on the palm of a hand. The hand was perfect.

From time to time I tried to explain to people why I bought the lampshade. After a while, I moved the lamp next to my bed and shut the bedroom door.

William Heyen

ROSEVILLE

Karen Dunkle had been browsing Paradise Mall's annual antique show and sale. She'd been looking carefully at a piece of Roseville pottery she was thinking of buying—a small blue bowl in the white rose pattern from the '40s, an object you could turn in your hands to feel the cyclic pattern of roses and vines in their imperishable frieze—but was that a chip in its base or just a natural kiln-fleck of some kind that wouldn't affect its value?—she'd been browsing and concentrating on white roses when Konrad Glimmerman, walking past her, slipped on a spot

of mustard and knocked her forward against three tiers of glassware and pottery while he himself fell not on his back with his
feet thrown up in front of him as is usually depicted in slapstick
cartoons, but, somehow, as we've observed, to Karen's side, his
left leg striking her in the back of her knees so that she seemed,
as the antique glassware and pottery swept over them in a wave
of shards and slivers, to be planning to sit on Konrad, which she
did. By the time the smashing and tinkling of breakage had
stopped, when the last carnival glass tumbler had rolled to a still-
point and the last cut-glass ashtray had stopped cracking and
spinning, Karen—the Roseville bowl that Konrad would later buy
for her intact in her hands—looked down at Konrad, who was
afraid to move, and said, "I don't believe we've been introduced."

To make a long story short, it is a week later. By now, Karen
and Konrad have exhausted all jokes about their first meeting,
have told and retold those few seconds to both circles of their
friends in such slow motion and with so many variations that it
seemed only natural to them that Karen should end up sitting on
Konrad's buttocks in Paradise Mall in the way she had, bits of
amethyst glass sequinned on her bouffant—miraculously, however
uncomfortable such fleeting notoriety might have made them,
neither had been even slightly hurt during this adventure—while
Konrad could think only of the dog ordure into which he must,
he thought, have stepped, could only hope that said dreck was
not beneath him at that very moment. After three dates, Karen
and Konrad have worn the story out. In fact, they swear to one
another that they will never again tell this story to themselves or
anyone else, that it will remain their own silent secret, that if they
ever argue or find themselves glum or heartbroken they will look
at one another and smirk, knowing what the other is remembering.

To make a very long story much shorter, however, we now see
them on their golden anniversary. As life would have it, it is after

dinner and frail Karen is standing at a microphone behind a three-tiered wedding cake at the Senior Center, which their children and friends have rented for the celebration. Just tall enough to see over the cake, she is looking out at this congregation and beginning to say a few words. Konrad, who broke his left hip a few months before, forgetful now and beginning to lose track of things, prone to wandering aimlessly about, stands up from his chair at the head table and begins walking behind Karen. A curve of blue begins to form in the back of his mind. He is thinking of telling a story.

Lex Williford

PENDERGAST'S
DAUGHTER

Leann and I were driving to her father's new A-frame on Lake Nacogdoches, and I was nervous about meeting her folks for the first time.

Relax, Leann said. Drink a few Old Mils with Dad, maybe catch a large mouth or two off the dock Saturday. When I got the nerve Sunday, she said, I could spring the news on the old man about wanting to marry his little girl. Then the two of us could get the hell out, head on back to Dallas. Lighten up, she kept saying.

When we got there her kid brother ran to my car, flinging his arms all around. An acre lot across a little inlet was being cleared, flat red clay and loblollies tied with red ribbons. A bulldozer was ramming one of the pines without much luck. Hurry, Leann's brother said.

The lake house was all glass in front so from the gravel drive we could see Mrs. Pendergast inside, slapping the old man's face. Once, twice, then again. She shouted something about him not having any goddamn imagination, about some girl, twenty-six years old, young enough to be his goddamn daughter. He took her flat palms rigid-faced, just stood there blinking at her. Then his face fell all apart, and he hit her in the sternum with his fist. She staggered back through the open door and up to the balcony rail as he hit her over and over again.

Do something, Leann shouted at me. But I just stood there. I just watched till the old man pushed his wife over the rail.

At the hospital in Lufkin I told Leann, I don't know what the hell happened to me. But then an intern came into the waiting room and said her mom would be all right, just some stitches, some bruised ribs.

Next week I must have left a hundred messages on Leann's answering machine. I'm sorry, they said, you got to believe me.

I remember we used to shower together every morning I stayed at her garage apartment in University Park. I'd slick her taut brown shoulders with Zest and I'd think, Jesus, this is good.

Kent Thompson

PONDEROSA

Jimmy's father said to come by the church, they should have a talk. Everybody knows what that means. But what his father said was that he had been out to the Ponderosa Restaurant on Saturday and there were all of Jimmy's classmates from Bible college with their wives and children and they were all happy, why wasn't he? He wanted Jimmy to get down on his knees and pray right there and Jimmy wouldn't and his father accused him of betraying his wife Linda and running around with that other woman—were these rumors true or untrue? They were untrue, said Jimmy. So his father said: do you have doubts? And Jimmy said he did, and then agreed to pray with his father. He decided to take the church at Mount Hebron and renounce the other woman—about whom he had lied to his father.

But then Linda came to his father the very next week to complain that Jimmy was cruel to her—he ignored her, and said cutting things to her, mocked her—was that any way to treat a Christian wife? Jimmy's father threw up his hands in despair. Was he expected to deal with everything? Were not his troubles with his own congregation enough?

He went over to see Jimmy with a shotgun in his hand, said it was only a symbol of God's potential wrath, he had no intention of using it, no, but it went off accidentally. Blew off half of Jimmy's jaw. It was only God's mercy that Jimmy didn't die—and afterwards Jimmy was a man possessed by the spirit of God. He and his father are on the road now with the Tabernacle Tent, bringing God's message as a team. His father tells the story and Jimmy, who can't talk anymore, sings—a melodious mourning sound which brings the sinners from the back rows to the front to be saved. God be praised!

Stuart Dybek

GOLD COAST

They wake simultaneously in a hotel room on the thirty-seventh floor, neither of them sure of the time, both still a little drunk, a little numb from the silence that has grown between them.

"Look at the sky! Look at the light!" she exclaims.

He's already seen it—how could he not have? The enormous bed faces a wall of windows. They've left the drapes open. The wall of windows now seems like a wall of sky, almost indigo, shot with iridescence as if veins of a newly discovered precious mineral have been exposed. It isn't dawn yet. It's still a gradation of night, but night with tomorrow already luminous behind it like the silver behind the glass of a cobalt mirror.

He can see the sky reflected in the windows of all the surrounding buildings that tower up to form the glass cliffs of the gold coast they've drifted to. He knows that every city has such strips, and he distrusts them. No matter how authentically elegant they might appear, he thinks of them as illusory, removed from the real life of cities, as places that are really no place, reflections floating like illuminated scum on the surface of a river. He remembers how, as teenagers, he and a buddy spent their nights exploring the gold coast of the city they'd grown up in, and the mixture of awe and contempt they'd felt toward it.

He no longer feels superior to gold coasts. He wonders how many of his fellow sleepers are sitting up as he is, silently peering out of high-rise rooms in which the drapes have been drawn open on tremendous windows, windows for giants, scaled to span the winking horizon of the city. He both envies those still sleeping peacefully and pities them for missing these nameless few moments of sky which he knows already will be unforgettable. He wonders which of those two emotions the future will reveal as the more accurate. Once, shortly after they'd become lovers, she told him, "I'm not sure if meeting you has been the most lucky or unlucky thing that's ever happened to me."

He had laughed.

"I wasn't kidding," she said.

"I know," he said, "I'm only laughing because that's exactly what I was thinking about meeting you."

"See. Maybe that's what happens when it's fate. One always feels what the other is feeling, at the same time, together." She laughed too.

"Kind of emotional telepathy, eh?"

"That makes it sound too glandular," she said in the teasing way she had that made for private jokes between them. "I'm not talking about something in the *glands*; I'm talking about something in the stars."

Now, beside him in bed, she whispers, "Why did we have to see this together?" It's not said cruelly. He understands what she means. She means they've seen this sky only because of one another; that it's something more between them to remember. And he knows that he doesn't need to answer, that it's as if he's merely overheard her speaking to herself, almost as if he isn't there any longer, as if she's awakened alone, at an unknown hour, along a gold coast.

MR. MUMSFORD

Bibs, the janitor, had never killed a man before. He'd raised rabbits as a boy and killed one now and then for supper. A quick blow to the back of the neck, and it was done. He was not a particularly intelligent man and was not suffering from guilt or any philosophical questions about what he was going to do. He had come to the small southern school as a janitor twenty-seven years ago. On his first day at school, he had worn a pair of old bib overalls and thus earned the nickname of Bibs. This was the reason he had come to kill the principal who was working late in his office down the hall. Earlier in the evening, Bibs had gone into the equipment room and picked out the largest baseball bat he could find. He then went and hid in a space between the green metal lockers that lined the hallways. At a little past ten the principal walked out of his office, locked it, and started down the hall. Bibs stepped out in front of him.

"Say, Bibs," asked the principal. "What are you doing here this time of night?"

Beads of sweat stood out on Bibs's forehead, and he clenched the bat with both hands. He was six feet tall, very black, and towered over the principal.

"I come to kill you," said Bibs.

"But why? What have I ever done to you?"

"Just what you called me is why!" said Bibs. "Nobody in this school, including you, has ever bothered to learn my real name. Onliest person knows my real name is that woman signs my check, and even she puts it in an envelope marked BIBS. The kids should learn my name in four years. Hell, I know more'n half of their names and where they live. This morning I stopped a couple of 'em and asked 'em did they know my real name, and they looked at me like I was crazy. That's why I come to kill you!"

The principal was a short man anyway, but now his shoulders slumped even further, and he looked sad and confused.

"Well," he said. "Well, what *is* your name?"

"Ralph Mumsford," said Bibs.

"Mumsford's a strange name for a black man to have," said the principal. "It's English, isn't it?"

"I don't know."

"You should look it up," said the principal. "You should go over to the school library and look it up. Say, lookee here, if I promise me and all my teachers call you by your real name from now on, will you not kill me?"

Bibs thought for a moment, seemed to waver, and then said, "Well, that seems fair. You do that, and I won't have to kill you." The principal looked tired.

"You been working too many hours," said Bibs. "A Christian man ought to always eat the supper meal with his wife."

The principal sighed and said, "I do believe you're right, Mr. Mumsford. I do believe you have a point there." Then he turned and walked down the dark corridor toward the green exit sign leading out to the playground.

Adrienne Clasky

FROM THE
FLOODLANDS

Here at the bottom of the country our windows drip with summer. The air is far too thick to breathe: This weekend seven people went for afternoon walks and drowned on the air. A boat crashed into a plane. The boat captain had slipped up above the horizon line by mistake, and is quoted in local papers as saying: "I didn't notice till I saw that 747 coming straight at me and I looked down to read the wind's direction on the waves and found them a whole lot lower down than I'd expected."

And we have had other problems with that horizon line. It

wobbles, for one thing. Some say the sky leaned so heavy with water against it that it stretched out of shape. Others say it is just a reaction to modern times, which all times are to it, and that it is having a harder and harder time keeping separate what should not be blended. It must have sagged up across the sky again last night because this morning it had pieces of clouds like tufts of cat hair stuck down the length of it. Later birds will come and pick it clean. Then they will open their immense wings in a crescendo of wind song against slick feathers. Their shadows will move like sharks through the water. Eventually they will land on a tangle of seaweed, thinking it is land. And they will land harder, thinking to find some solidity, but will only tangle their ankles, ankles so thin and fragile it breaks your heart to look at them, tangled in those green, slimy chains, and they will open their beaks to the sky, to call to it, beg for its dry white rush, but find only mud's cousin, and their beaks will be wide with wonder and supplication as they go down, and down . . .

The birds are not talked about in church here on Sunday. What is talked about is the drought. What could the rest of the country have been doing to bring this down on themselves? After services, two more pews are moved out. Water has begun seeping under the walls and the wooden pews expand. They are softer though, and your behind leaves an impression when you wade up to kiss the preacher's knees and send through him a message to Jesus: Please forgive them, Lord. They meant no harm. They were only thirsty. Of course, thirst is no excuse, is, in fact, *the* great sin. Even Jesus committed it, so I hear tell, those last hours on the Cross.

After church one day, we all met in the town hall for a town meeting. A Yankee had come to speak to us, a corn farmer from Illinois. His lips were caked with cracking skin. Most of the blue had evaporated from his eyes—they were slices of a cloudless sky white with heat, blowing this way and that around the room. He had to do that to keep track of his audience, since the folding chairs on which we sat bobbed and rocked and whirled in the current of the tea-colored water across the floor.

"We have done nothing up there, I swear it," he said, and held up his great hands. Shoals of skin fell from his arms, melted into the water. "Nothing different, anyway, nothing no one else doesn't do." His voice broke apart then, and his face, and I suppose he was crying, but who can tell for sure? There were no tears . . . And in his scraping, parching voice he said, "Just a few drops, a bucketful, maybe . . ." And the sound turned to powder in his throat. "Well," a neighbor lady said later, "you can just listen to *that* for so long."

Needless to say, our town refused his request. It is never a good idea to offer the hand of help to one who needs it too badly. It is like landing on seaweed.

The whole day depressed me, so I climbed onto my air mattress and floated down Lake Street to the place where the shore used to be and I watched the sunken sun throb with peach and apricot and raspberry and every wet, fresh color any human has ever named, and I saw how that line of division, that "horizon" line, was not wobbling erratically as our town believed, but moved in quavers as regular and predictable as the pulse of a heart's string.

Allan Gurganus

A PUBLIC
DENIAL

Despite persistent rumors to the contrary, my grandfather did not die driving a Toyota across his pond. As I will demonstrate, this is a bald mistruth. Admittedly, he had become somewhat senile or eccentric in recent years. In view of the attempted firing of the courthouse cannon last July, it would be foolish to state otherwise. But certain exaggerations now in circulation are unfair to his family's memory of him and must be corrected.

While bizarre, many of the stories about his attempts to secure

the local Toyota dealership are true. Just after Corona wagons
were introduced in this country, he bought one for use on his
farms. For reasons none of us will ever know, he began to take
an interest, a very active interest, in the well-being of the Toyota
company. He decided at age seventy-one to become the local
dealer for the car, but because of his advanced years and idio-
syncrasies, the franchise was withheld. He bought three more
Toyotas, either to endear himself to the home office or maybe
out of pure enthusiasm. These, Corona convertibles, he gave to
grandchildren. (One is still in the author's possession and running
like a top.) But not even his extra purchases brought so much as
a discount from the mother office.

At this point in Grandfather's quest for the franchise, he staged
the much-discussed "pond-drive." Having read in the owner's man-
ual that the Toyota is more perfectly watertight than almost any
other car, he decided to personally demonstrate and document
this fact, thus winning the long-sought-after approval of Toyota
International. To his farm near Little Easonburg, he summoned
six tenant farmers and one twelve-year-old grandson. They were
stationed at five-feet intervals along the pond bank, each man
equipped with a loaded camera borrowed or bought for the oc-
casion. The pond itself is a small one dug for irrigation purposes
in 1959. My grandfather, a conservationist long before it was
fashionable, had at one time stocked the pond with bass which
shiftless tenant farmers are said to have fished out and eaten before
any achieved maturity.

His theory was that the rotating rear tires would propel the car
through the water. He evidently drove it slowly down the east
bank, honking the horn: a prearranged signal to "Aim all cameras."
Eased into the water, the car actually floated, moving slowly to
the center of the pond. Once there, it veered toward shore, the
speedometer registering 110 mph while the vehicle advanced at

only about 3 mph through the water. Some moisture did seep in, but hardly enough to sink the car, as many have falsely reported. The experiment, in short, was an overwhelming success. When the Toyota containing my grandfather finally scrambled up the opposite bank, the six tenant farmers and one grandson, the writer's first cousin, are said to have let out a spontaneous cheer.

It was immediately afterwards, while taking the car for a quick land drive—toward the nearest public telephone some two miles away—that the fatal accident occurred. Maneuvering the curve along Bank Road, he evidently lost control of the car. It crashed over a low bridge and into a farm pond much deeper than his own. He had lowered the car's windows, to dry what little water had originally seeped in. With all the windows open, his Corona did not float long this time. He went down with it.

I have given all these specifics to point out that the pond in which he drowned was more than a mile and a half from the original site of his *successful* experiment. This, I hope, will put an end to rumors that his death was somehow foolhardy. Though the "pond-drive" photographs proved inconclusive (exhaust fumes, of the sky, etc.), we still have the witnesses' spoken accounts. In short, the man died having proved something which is more than most of us can say. Toyota International, hearing of his death, sent our family a letter signed by a vice-president of that company. It expressed gratitude for Grandfather's "pioneering consumer spirit," and went on to say, "We could certainly use more customers with his brand of courage and devotion." This, I hope, will finally quiet local cynics and permit his widow, bereaved children, and grandchildren to live normal lives again.

Carol Edelstein

232-9979

Maybe calling you was a mistake. I could hear the kids. I do not know how I will begin to admit to what I have done.

I suppose I will start by parking next to your house. But immediately I begin to imagine road construction that will make this impossible. I will find a place, though, even if it means the Quick Stop parking lot. This won't be any quick stop, though, if you are home, and answer my knock. I have nothing to say, but I think I'm going to need a lot of time to say it.

I don't know how far back I should go. There have been recent volcanic eruptions on Venus. The newspaper said "recent," as defined by scientists, is "300,000 to several million" years ago. But I guess I'll start with three winters ago, December 19 to be exact, when your husband and I got into our first accident. Car accident. Nobody hurt, but addresses were exchanged, license plate numbers, insurance information—and I'll admit, I couldn't help it, I noted your husband's eye color. Hazel.

Nothing else would have happened between us if three weeks later I had not returned the box of farina with flour-beetles to Bonno's Food Warehouse where I don't usually shop because of incidents like the above and also my ex–sister-in-law works there and we have never seen eye-to-eye. How could I have intended for your husband to be right ahead of me in the checkout, buying formula and plastic diapers? The first thing I noticed was his neck brace, but then, when I saw who he was, I had to inquire. If I was going to get smacked with a lawsuit I wanted to know about it. Wouldn't you?

But even then nothing else might have happened if, on January 16, my downstairs neighbor Matty had not smoked in bed. I remember the date clearly because I had taken off work that morning to bring my mother in for a root canal. She turned out to be allergic to the ether or whatever it is they made her suck and she practically died in the chair.

I've lectured Matty about smoking safely in bed but she doesn't learn. She practically burned down the hallway, which needed it, but if it weren't for your husband and his men it could have gone further.

I was unintentionally in my yellow robe, kind of shivering, and I said, "Hank Henkins!" because by then I knew him by name.

"Hank Henkins! That can't be you!" Of course, I was pleased to see him under those circumstances—you would've been, too.

And I'll admit it even if he doesn't—that's when I think he first noticed *my* eye color. Just for the record, they're blue.

This is the silly speech I am driving around with, although I have not yet made the call. I have Elly Henkins' number and I have driven by her house frequently enough to know she is home. The garage door is open, and the twins' stroller, in the middle of the sidewalk, is in a suggestive position. It is time to make a speech of some kind. I am over-my-head in love with Hank Henkins, and it won't wait until Kathy and Pam are grown up. It won't even wait until they are at least prom age, which Hank and me were both trying for. I thought we could have the longest flirt in history with no dire consequences, but now a thing has happened and I can't wait.

Raymond Carver

THE FATHER

The baby lay in a basket beside the bed, dressed in a white bonnet and sleeper. The basket had been newly painted and tied with ice-blue ribbons and padded with blue quilts. The three little sisters and the mother, who had just gotten out of bed and was still not herself, and the grandmother all stood around the baby, watching it stare and sometimes raise its fist to its mouth. He did not smile or laugh, but now and then he blinked his eyes and flicked his tongue back and forth through his lips when one of the girls rubbed his chin.

The father was in the kitchen and could hear them playing with the baby.

"Who do you love, baby?" Phyllis said and tickled his chin.

"He loves us all," Phyllis said, "but he really loves Daddy because Daddy's a boy too!"

The grandmother sat down on the edge of the bed and said, "Look at its little arm! So fat. And those little fingers! Just like its mother."

"Isn't he sweet?" the mother said. "So healthy, my little baby." And bending over, she kissed the baby on its forehead and touched the cover over its arm. "We love him too."

"But who does he look like, who does he look like?" Alice cried, and they all moved up closer around the basket to see who the baby looked like.

"He has pretty eyes," Carol said.

"*All* babies have pretty eyes," Phyllis said.

"He has his grandfather's lips," the grandmother said. "Look at those lips."

"I don't know . . ." the mother said. "I wouldn't say."

"The nose! The nose!" Alice cried.

"What about his nose?" the mother asked.

"It looks like somebody's nose," the girl answered.

"No, I don't know," the mother said. "I don't think so."

"Those lips . . ." the grandmother murmured. "Those little fingers . . ." she said, uncovering the baby's hand and spreading out its fingers.

"Who does the baby look like?"

"He doesn't look like anybody," Phyllis said. And they moved even closer.

"*I* know! *I* know!" Carol said. "He looks like *Daddy!*" Then they looked closer at the baby.

"But who does Daddy *look* like?" Phyllis asked.

"Who does Daddy *look* like?" Alice repeated, and they all at once looked through to the kitchen where the father was sitting at the table with his back to them.

"Why, nobody!" Phyllis said and began to cry a little.

"Hush," the grandmother said and looked away and then back at the baby.

"Daddy doesn't look like *anybody!*" Alice said.

"But he has to look like *somebody*," Phyllis said, wiping her eyes with one of the ribbons. And all of them except the grandmother looked at the father, sitting at the table.

He had turned around in his chair and his face was white and without expression.

Lon Otto

LOVE POEMS

He has written her a St. Valentine's Day love poem. It is very beautiful; it expresses, embodies a passionate, genuine emotion, emotion of a sort he hardly realized himself capable of, tenderness that is like the tenderness of a better man. At the same time, the imagery is hard, diamond clear, the form intricate yet unobtrusive. He says the poem out loud to himself over and over. He cannot believe it, it is so good. It is the best poem he has ever written.

He will mail it to her tonight. She will open it as soon as it arrives, cleverly timed, on St. Valentine's Day. She will be floored, she will be blown away by its beauty and passion. She will put it away with his other letters, loving him for it, as she loves him for his other letters. She will not show it to anyone, for she is a private person, which is one of the qualities he loves in her.

After he has mailed the poem to her, written out in his interesting hand, he types up a copy for his own files. He decides to send a copy to one of the more prestigious literary magazines, one into which he has not yet been admitted. He hesitates about the dedication, which could lead to embarrassment, among other things, with his wife. In the end he omits the dedication. In the end he decides to give a copy also to his wife. In the end he sends a copy also to a woman he knows in England, a poet who really understands his work. He writes out a copy for her, dedicated to her initials. It will reach her a few days late, she will think of him thinking of her a few days before St. Valentine's Day.

NIGHT

He woke up. He thought he could hear their child's breathing in the next room, the near-silent, smooth sound of air in and out.

He touched his wife. The room was too dark to let him see her, but he felt her movement, the shift of blanket and sheet.

"Listen," he whispered.

"Yesterday," she mumbled. "Why not yesterday," and she moved back into sleep.

He listened harder; though he could hear his wife's breath,

thick and heavy next to him, there was beneath this the thin frost of his child's breathing.

The hardwood floor was cold beneath his feet. He held out a hand in front of him, and when he touched the doorjamb, he paused, listened again, heard the life in his child.

His fingertips led him along the hall and to the next room. Then he was in the doorway of a room as dark, as hollow as his own. He cut on the light.

The room, of course, was empty. They had left the bed just as their child had made it, the spread merely thrown over bunched and wrinkled sheets, the pillow crooked at the head. The small blue desk was littered with colored pencils and scraps of construction paper, a bottle of white glue.

He turned off the light and listened. He heard nothing, then backed out of the room and moved down the hall, back to his room, his hands at his sides, his fingertips helpless.

This happened each night, like a dream, but not.

Kristin Andrychuk

MANDY SHUPE

I'm thinking about you today, Mandy Shupe. Thinking about you dancing on a picnic table at Crystal Beach. Wondering about the true story and how that image often comes to mind when things are bad for me.

My mother told me about you when I was a little girl. Why, I don't know. Something to do with self-control?

What sank in was that Mandy Shupe, a Mennonite, left the church and danced naked on a picnic table at Crystal Beach. Crystal Beach, longest roller coaster in the world, so the sign said.

Bright pink castle fun house and a crowded beach. Blacks from Buffalo, Negroes we called them then. Flashy clothes and an aura of perfume, though Mother said they were poor, lived in slums, weren't treated well. Didn't look poor to me. And the gangs of teenagers, slicked back, duck-tailed hair (duck's ass the less polite kids at school called it). The girls in short shorts or tight skirts showing off all they had as Mother would say. The smells of popcorn, dust, and sweat mixing with the screams from the roller coaster and loop-de-loop. The dance hall with its chandeliers, dance band, laughing couples.

I pictured you in your long gray clothes leaving the Mennonite church, walking the three miles to Crystal Beach with a man. Even then I knew somehow a man was involved. I saw you climbing up on the bench of the picnic table, the man giving you his hand.

You take off the big gray bonnet and the small white organdy underbonnet. Lay them neatly on the bench. With a shake of your head, uncoiling your dark hair. Removing the long gray dress, the chemise, and the heavy flannel petticoat. Unlacing the corset. Slipping down the hand-sewn cotton bloomers. Folding each garment neatly there on the bench. Stepping from bench to table.

The dancing. Slowly at first, then faster and faster as the people cheer.

When I grew up I knew this story was preposterous and asked my mother what she had told me as a child.

The updated version was you had left the church several years before and had become a loose woman. You were drunk out at Crystal Beach, with a man, and you did dance naked on a picnic table.

Well, I had the "with a man" part right, but I'm disappointed it took several years after you left the church. Though by now I can understand why it did. Disappointed by the drunk part, too, though I wonder about that. The people telling the story were teetotalers. If you'd had a drink, you'd be drunk.

I still see you, Mandy, in full control, with a little smile on your face as you take off your clothes, which maybe weren't really Mennonite clothes, but in your head I bet they were. I see you dancing, dancing through the warm, brightly lit night.

Tom Hawkins

WEDDING
NIGHT

I have worked at this bus station magazine stand since nineteen fifty three, waiting for the right girl to come along. When I took this job, the paint on that wall over there was new; it was a light green color then. The servicemen from the Korean War would stop and buy cigarettes, and I learned the insignia from the Army, Coast Guard, Navy, and Marines.

Once I was held up by a stocky white man in a brown jacket. Showed me the two teeth he had left in his head and the barrel of a little tape-wrapped automatic pointed at my heart. I gave him all the dough but never felt scared. Way I saw it, he was just like me, and I could die behind that counter and just walk away inside his skin, with a few dollars to spend. We were all one thing. So I handed him the money, feeling richer right away—three hundred twenty-three dollars—and let him get away before I called the cops.

I heard they never caught him, then I heard they caught him in another state—Utah I think—and then I heard they found him dead in an airport parking lot in Kansas. I don't know. He may be out there yet. He may be back. May hold me up tonight, or just shoot me dead, or both.

Anything can happen in the bus station. In the nineteen-sixties, we had what we called the hippies, young people in ragged get-ups. They used to sleep all over the furniture in sleeping bags, with packs and rolled-up tents.

That's when I began to think that the right girl might come along after all, some girl who'd grown tired of the long-haired boys, and tired of the road, and walk home with me and hold my hand, and curl up with me in my bed and on my squeaky springs. I kept an eye out. One day I saw a young lady: she looked so long-tired and in need of a friend. I bought her a sandwich and coffee and a peanut-butter cup. I bought her some aspirin and a pint of milk, fingernail clippers and a souvenir shirt.

I told her I had a place where she could come to rest and stay, as long as she might want. I told her it wasn't fancy and wasn't but one room, but what was mine was hers. I knew it was clean. I'd cleaned it up the day before when I saw this girl hanging around.

She stroked my hair and said my heart was full of love. She said she had to sleep about twelve hours and then she'd go away. I took her home. She slumped down on the bed and cried—told me I was "so very kind." And then she slept like the dead. I lay down on the floor beside her, where I said I'd stay. In the middle of the night I woke up on fire, and the room was turning. I couldn't think. The air turned furry, where I crept up and slid in bed beside her, that girl still completely dressed. She breathed like the sea. I touched her skin, just her skin inside her clothes. She really never woke, just sighed and turned. In the morning when I woke up in the bed, she was gone.

I've worked here since nineteen fifty three, waiting for the right girl to come along. I guess she did. Some good marriages don't last long.

Bruce Eason

THE
APPALACHIAN
TRAIL

Today she tells me that it is her ambition to walk the
Appalachian Trail, from Maine to Georgia. I ask how far it is. She
says, "Some two thousand miles."

"No, no," I reply, "you must mean two hundred, not two
thousand."

"I mean two thousand," she says, "more or less, two thousand
miles long. I've done some reading too, about people who've
completed the journey. It's amazing."

"Well, you've read the wrong stuff," I say. "You should've read about the ones that didn't make it. Those stories are more important. Why they gave up is probably why you shouldn't be going."

"I don't care about that, I'm going," she says with a determined look. "My mind is made up."

"Listen," I say, reaching for words to crush her dream. "Figure it out, figure out the time. How long will it take to walk two thousand miles?" I leap up to get a pen and paper. Her eyes follow me, like a cat that is ready to pounce.

"Here now," I say, pen working, setting numbers deep into the paper. "Let's say you walk, on average, some twenty miles a day. That's twenty into two thousand, right? It goes one hundred times. And so, one hundred equals exactly one hundred years. It'll take you one hundred years!"

"Don't be stupid," she says. "One hundred *days*, not years."

"Oh, yeah, okay, days," I mumble. I was never good at math. I feel as if someone has suddenly twisted an elastic band around my forehead. I crumple the paper, turn to her and say, "So if it's one hundred days, what is that? How many months?"

"A little over three." She calculates so fast that I agree without thinking. "Fine, but call it four months," I say, "because there's bound to be some delay: weather, shopping for supplies, maybe first-aid treatments. You never know, you have to make allowances."

"All right, I make allowances, four months."

What have I done? It sounds as if all of this nonsense is still in full swing. *Say more about the time.* "Okay," I say, "so where do we get the time to go? What about my job? What about my responsibilities, *your* responsibilities too? What about—?"

"What about I send you a postcard when I finish the trip," she says, leaving the room.

I sit there mouthing my pen. I hear her going down the basement steps. Pouting now, I think. Sulking. She knows she's wrong about this one.

"Seen my backpack?" she calls from below. God, she's really going to do it. "Next to mine," I say. "On the shelf beside the freezer."

I am angry with myself. She has had her way, won without even trying. "Take mine down too," I blurt out. "You can't expect to walk the Appalachian Trail all alone." I stare at my feet. "Sorry," I say to them both, "I'm really sorry about all of this."

Russell Edson

DINNER TIME

An old man sitting at a table was waiting for his wife to serve dinner. He heard her beating a pot that had burned her. He hated the sound of a pot when it was beaten, for it advertised its pain in such a way that made him wish to inflict more of same. And he began to punch at his own face, and his knuckles were red. How he hated red knuckles, that blaring color, more self-important than the wound.

He heard his wife drop the entire dinner on the kitchen floor with a curse. For as she was carrying it in it had burned her thumb.

He heard the forks and spoons, the cups and platters all cry at once as they landed on the kitchen floor. How he hated a dinner that, once prepared, begins to burn one to death, and as if that weren't enough, screeches and roars as it lands on the floor, where it belongs anyway.

He punched himself again and fell on the floor.

When he came awake again he was quite angry, and so he punched himself again and felt dizzy. Dizziness made him angry, and so he began to hit his head against the wall, saying, now get real dizzy if you want to get dizzy. He slumped to the floor.

Oh, the legs won't work, eh? . . . He began to punch his legs. He had taught his head a lesson and now he would teach his legs a lesson.

Meanwhile he heard his wife smashing the remaining dinnerware and the dinnerware roaring and shrieking.

He saw himself in the mirror on the wall. Oh, mock me, will you. And so he smashed the mirror with a chair, which broke. Oh, don't want to be a chair no more, too good to be sat on, eh? He began to beat the pieces of the chair.

He heard his wife beating the stove with an ax. He called, when're we going to eat? as he stuffed a candle into his mouth.

When I'm good and ready, she screamed.

Want me to punch your bun? he screamed.

Come near me and I'll kick an eye out of your head.

I'll cut your ears off.

I'll give you a slap right in the face.

I'll kick you right in the breadbasket.

I'll break you in half.

The old man finally ate one of his hands. The old woman said, damn fool, whyn't you cook it first? You go on like a beast—you know I have to subdue the kitchen every night, otherwise it'll cook me and serve me to the mice on my best china. And you know what small eaters they are; next would come the flies, and how I hate flies in my kitchen.

The old man swallowed a spoon. Okay, said the old woman, now we're short one spoon.

The old man, growing angry, swallowed himself.

Okay, said the woman, now you've done it.

Luisa Valenzuela

VISION OUT
OF THE CORNER
OF ONE EYE

I t's true, he put his hand on my ass and I was about to scream bloody murder when the bus passed by a church and he crossed himself. He's a good sort after all, I said to myself. Maybe he didn't do it on purpose or maybe his right hand didn't know what his left hand was up to. I tried to move farther back in the bus—searching for explanations is one thing and letting yourself be pawed is another—but more passengers got on and there was no way I could do it. My wiggling to get out of his reach only let him get a better hold on me and even fondle me. I was nervous and finally moved over. He moved over, too. We passed by another church but he didn't notice it and when he raised his hand to his face it was to wipe the sweat off his forehead. I watched him out of the corner of one eye, pretending that nothing was happening, or at any rate not making him think I liked it. It was impossible to move a step farther and he began jiggling me. I decided to get even and put my hand on his behind. A few blocks later I got separated from him. Then I was swept along by the passengers getting off the bus and now I'm sorry I lost him so suddenly because there were only 7,400 pesos in his wallet and I'd have gotten more out of him if we'd been alone. He seemed affectionate. And very generous.

Translated by Helen Lane

I GET SMART

I tell him I'm thinking about getting a new cat.

"No way," he says, like this is not negotiable. As if I haven't paid half the rent since grad school, and all the cat costs, including the spiffy new cat door installed next to the fridge.

I say I've been to the Animal Rescue League and they have seventeen adorable kittens—all colors. "You get to pick the color," I say.

"Hold it," he says. He lines up his sharp accountant's pencil across the top of his crossword, cracks the knuckles of his right

---

hand. "I do not want another cat. What's wrong with the three we've got?"

The three we've got hear our voices rising and pad into the kitchen to see what's going on. The Persian, Jeanette, threads back and forth through my legs, her long hair flying, while gray-striped Fitzhugh leaps onto the fridge and blinks down at us. Sweetpeach, the calico, jumps into my lap and kneads my chenille stomach. Not a cat goes near Roy.

"There's nothing wrong with the three we've got," I say.

"So forget a new cat," he says, and turns back to his crossword.

I scratch behind Sweetpeach's ears to make her purr, and finish my Sunday morning pot of real coffee. I've already finished a Xerox of Roy's crossword and I know just which word will hang him up.

Next Sunday during crosswords and coffee I make the introductions. I say, "Well, we now have three new cats."

Roy gets macho, points his pencil at me. "Where the hell—I told you . . ."

I tell him, calm down, don't get all riled up before you meet them. But his voice rises in spite of my attempts to keep the peace. So my voice rises, too, as in any proper duet, and sure enough the cats come by.

"This is Savannah," I say as Sweetpeach appears, her tail whipping the air, weighing my distress.

Roy snorts and I try to remember if he ever called the cats by name.

"And that is Joe Namath." I point to Fitzhugh eyeing us from the top of the fridge where he is poised in a three-point stance. "He never acted like a Fitzhugh," I say. "Parents should change their kids' names every few years for just that reason. Or give them nicknames."

"It's the other way around," Roy says. "Kids named Moonbeam, Taj Mahal, and Free are now calling themselves Susie, Pat, and Jim."

"You see," I say.

"No," he says. "I don't." His eyes refuse to focus on me or the cats. He lets his coffee get cold.

Jeanette springs onto the counter and highsteps over the stove to the window where she watches the action at our veggie neighbor's high-tech cat-proof birdfeeder. I tell Roy he'll be sure to remember her name. "You're always saying 'what a pill.' So that's Pillow."

"Don't do this," he says.

"So we have not one but three new cats," I say, burying my nose in Savannah's spotted fur. She's as limp as her new name and warm. Her cat's eyes seem to remember hot African grasslands and prey ten times larger than she is.

"We have three cats—period," Roy says. He has a way of making syntax dull.

"Three new cats," I say.

"Bull!" Roy's pencil bounces high like a cat toy.

Joe Namath jumps from the fridge onto the table and skids into Roy's crossword. Roy's tackle is rough and Joe Namath spits as Roy tosses him into the dining room. Pillow, the bird-watcher, cantilevers one ear around to hear when to abandon her post. Roy scoops his pencil from the floor and taps it on his crossword in disgust. Three words earlier he went wrong, but he won't know this until I tell him. I shiver Savannah off my lap and leave to shower.

During the next two weeks, Roy gets mad every time I call the cats by their new names. But he is more mad that Savannah, Joe

Namath, and Pillow take to their names so quickly. It's all in the tone of voice, I tell him.

I get happy with my new cats.

After a couple of months I get smart. Come Sunday breakfast it isn't Roy filling in the crossword; it's a new man—better with words and cats—named Ralph.

TRUE LOVE

They met at a national entomology conference. To his eye, she was a woman of extraordinary physical grace and beauty, the last thing he expected to find at a professional conference.

He was struck by her slender, hairless forearms, the delicate curve of her neck, the proud way she carried her rather small head.

His tall thin frame and slightly bulging eyes reminded her of the subjects of her first highly successful entomological research project. It was a strong and fond memory. The project had established her reputation for creative insectology.

He approached her during the cocktail hour after the first day's papers.

"Hello," he said, "I'm Lloyd Gaynor."

"Gaynor? Oh, yes. Termites."

He was pleased.

Her name was Phyllis Turner and he knew and admired her work on fire ants. Fortuitously, he was seated next to her at the dinner. Their mutual attraction was very strong, so strong that their exchanges took on a quality of escalation, advancing their intimacy in a series of minute but rapid steps, a breathless spiral like a ritual dance.

An attraction strong enough to evoke real fear.

A revelation occurred over the mocha bombe and espresso that excited her more than she cared to show. She realized that as part of the research he was describing in termite neurobiology he had developed a computer model that could save her six months in her statistical analysis of fire ant brain function. She expressed her interest in a low key, oblique way. He was encouraging but noncommittal.

Shortly after the dinner, by unspoken agreement, they ascended in the hotel elevator to her floor and entered her room. They undressed without speaking, he in the bathroom, she in the bedroom.

He entered the bedroom and paused, standing beside the bed. She stood naked across the bed from him. They examined each other's pale, slender, almost hairless bodies.

He spoke first.

"The female praying mantis is nearsighted and dangerous. When the male is impelled to mate, he approaches her slowly and with great caution, sometimes waiting motionless for up to twenty minutes before the next short advance. When he finally summons the courage to dash forward and mount her from the rear, she typically responds by twisting her upper body around and biting off his head. This act quite literally removes his innate fear of her, since it removes the neurons and ganglia in which that fear resides. He then copulates to a successful conclusion and dies, presumably as happily as any creature can without its head. After he dies, she eats the rest of him."

He paused and looked at her expectantly. His long thin penis extended out and upward with mute pink urgency.

When she spoke, she used the same light didactic tone as he.

"The female empid fly also has a nasty habit of eating the male when he approaches her during mating season. To divert her from this purpose, the male typically finds a morsel of food and wraps it elaborately in a silk balloon formed by his glandular secretions. The time it takes the female to unwrap his gift is often long enough for him to copulate successfully and escape unscathed. But in one empid species, whether through cleverness, laziness, or just bad faith, the male fails to put any food inside the balloon. The female is hoodwinked into copulation with an empty promise."

These things they said to each other were well known to both, as indeed they were to any first-year graduate student of entomology.

There was a pause after she spoke. They continued to stare at each other. It could have gone either way.

Then they fell upon each other.

Carolyn Forché

THE COLONEL

What you have heard is true. I was in his house. His
wife carried a tray of coffee and sugar. His daughter filed her
nails, his son went out for the night. There were daily papers, pet
dogs, a pistol on the cushion beside him. The moon swung bare
on its black cord over the house. On the television was a cop
show. It was in English. Broken bottles were embedded in the
walls around the house to scoop the kneecaps from a man's legs
or cut his hands to lace. On the windows there were gratings like
those in liquor stores. We had dinner, rack of lamb, good wine,

a gold bell was on the table for calling the maid. The maid brought green mangoes, salt, a type of bread. I was asked how I enjoyed the country. There was a brief commercial in Spanish. His wife took everything away. There was some talk then of how difficult it had become to govern. The parrot said hello on the terrace. The colonel told it to shut up, and pushed himself from the table. My friend said to me with his eyes: say nothing. The colonel returned with a sack used to bring groceries home. He spilled many human ears on the table. They were like dried peach halves. There is no other way to say this. He took one of them in his hands, shook it in our faces, dropped it into a water glass. It came alive there. I am tired of fooling around he said. As for the rights of anyone, tell your people they can go fuck themselves. He swept the ears to the floor with his arm and held the last of his wine in the air. Something for your poetry, no? he said. Some of the ears on the floor caught this scrap of his voice. Some of the ears on the floor were pressed to the ground.

Julia Alvarez

SNOW

Our first year in New York we rented a small apartment with a Catholic school nearby, taught by the Sisters of Charity, hefty women in long black gowns and bonnets that made them look peculiar, like dolls in mourning. I liked them a lot, especially my grandmotherly fourth grade teacher, Sister Zoe. I had a lovely name, she said, and she had me teach the whole class how to pronounce it. *Yo-lan-da*. As the only immigrant in my class, I was put in a special seat in the first row by the window, apart from the other children so that Sister Zoe could tutor me without disturbing them. Slowly, she enunciated the new words I was to repeat: *laundromat, cornflakes, subway, snow.*

Soon I picked up enough English to understand *holocaust* was in the air. Sister Zoe explained to a wide-eyed classroom what was happening in Cuba. Russian missiles were being assembled, trained supposedly on New York City. President Kennedy, looking worried too, was on the television at home, explaining we might have to go to war against the Communists. At school, we had air-raid drills: an ominous bell would go off and we'd file into the hall, fall to the floor, cover our heads with our coats, and imagine our hair falling out, the bones in our arms going soft. At home, Mami and my sisters and I said a rosary for world peace. I heard new vocabulary: *nuclear bomb, radioactive fallout, bomb shelter.* Sister Zoe explained how it would happen. She drew a picture of a mushroom on the blackboard and dotted a flurry of chalkmarks for the dusty fallout that would kill us all.

The months grew cold, November, December. It was dark when I got up in the morning, frosty when I followed my breath to school. One morning as I sat at my desk daydreaming out the window, I saw dots in the air like the ones Sister Zoe had drawn—random at first, then lots and lots. I shrieked, "Bomb! Bomb!" Sister Zoe jerked around, her full black skirt ballooning as she hurried to my side. A few girls began to cry.

But then Sister Zoe's shocked look faded. "Why, Yolanda dear, that's snow!" She laughed. "Snow."

"Snow," I repeated. I looked out the window warily. All my life I had heard about the white crystals that fell out of American skies in the winter. From my desk I watched the fine powder dust the sidewalk and parked cars below. Each flake was different, Sister Zoe said, like a person, irreplaceable and beautiful.

David Foster Wallace

EVERYTHING
IS GREEN

She says I do not care if you believe me or not, it is
the truth, go on and believe what you want to. So it is for sure
that she is lying, when it is the truth she will go crazy trying to
get you to believe her. So I feel like I know.

She lights up and looks off away from me, looking sly with her
cigarette through a wet window, and I can not feel what to say.

I say Mayfly I can not feel what to do or say or believe you
any more. But there is things I know. I know I am older and you
are not. And I give to you all I got to give you, with my hands

and my heart both. Every thing that is inside me I have gave you. I have been keeping it together and working steady every day. I have made you the reason I got for what I always do. I have tried to make a home to give to you, for you to be in, and for it to be nice.

I light up myself then I throw the match in the sink with other matches and dishes and a sponge and such things.

I say Mayfly my heart has been down the road and back for you but I am forty-eight years old. It is time I have got to not let things just carry me by any more. I got to use some time that is still mine to try to make every thing feel right. I got to try to feel how I need to. In me there is needs which you can not even see any more, because there is too many needs in you in the way.

She does not say any thing and I look at her window and I can feel that she knows. I know about it, and she shifts her self on my sofa lounger. She brings her legs up underneath her in some shorts.

I say it really does not matter what I seen or what I think I seen. That is not it any more. I know I am older and you are not. But now I am feeling like there is all of me going out to you and nothing of you coming back any more.

Her hair is up with a barrette and pins and her chin is in her hand, it's early, she looks like she is dreaming out at the clean light through the wet window over my sofa lounger.

Everything is green she says. Look how green it all is Mitch. How can you say the things you say you feel like when every thing outside is green like it is.

The window over the sink of my kitchenette is cleaned off from the hard rain last night, and it is a morning with sun, it is still early, and there is a mess of green out. The trees are green and some grass out past the speed bumps is green and slicked down. But every thing is not green. The other trailers are not green, and my card table out with puddles in lines and beer cans and butts floating in the ashtrays is not green, or my truck, or the gravel of the lot, or the Big Wheel toy that is on its side under a clothesline without no clothes on it by the next trailer, where the guy has got him some kids.

Everything is green she is saying. She is whispering it and the whisper is not to me no more I know.

I chuck my smoke and turn hard from the morning outside with the taste of something true in my mouth. I turn hard toward her in the light on the sofa lounger.

She is looking outside, from where she is sitting, and I look at her, and there is something in me that can not close up in that looking. Mayfly has a body. And she is my morning. Say her name.

DRAFT HORSE

When he was a kid growing up in Fargo, he used to walk from the barn to the house, thirty below, his breath steaming out and then flowing past his face. On those mornings he could hear the way the cows seemed to brush together in the cold, and imagined he could hear them at night when the temperature dropped even lower. From his bedroom it sounded like their hides were made of metal, how each hair had frozen on their backs and was rasping against the others.

And he remembered the way the sun used to look coming in

through a quarter inch of frost on the single pane window. It would break up, splashing into a prism on the walls. He would wake and hold his finger to the cold window, then come back later in the day from school and find his fingerprints perfectly preserved in ice.

Each day in the cold, each month when it never got above freezing, he wondered how the sun could shine and not warm him. He would stand for as long as he could and watch his shadow move in an arc in front of his body. The cold would begin in his shoes then work its way up the inside of his legs. Then his fingers would go numb and he would be dancing in the January sun, his shadow cavorting on top of the snow.

Each morning he would have to go to the cows. There would be the smell of heat rising from their bodies mixed with the smell of hot manure, steaming below them. He shoveled the warm odor sifting like mist into his nostrils.

Sometimes when he shoveled, he remembered the old stories about the cold. Men freezing in their sleep. Or how the water would freeze in mid-air after you threw it out of the bucket.

After he washed the manure smell from his skin with pure castile soap, he would always go back into his room and look for a long time at the photograph of his grandfather on Rogers Lake. It was 1925. There were several men standing around a burning horse carcass on the ice. The flames rose black and thick into the February sky. The horse, a huge Belgian mare, had slipped hauling ice on the lake.

He remembered the way his grandfather described bringing the horse down. How he slipped the barrel into her ear as if it were a finger, he said. He had wanted to leave her on the ice, let the cold take her but his brother had insisted she be shot and burned on the spot where she failed.

So they put her down. One shot. Then Uncle Ike doused her

with gasoline. Someone, perhaps his grandfather, had touched the match to the mottled hair and the horse rose in flame like a storm. When they all stepped back someone took the picture. In the right corner of the photograph near the wagon you could see small icicles beginning to form on the ice blocks piled four high, the men holding their arms to shield them from the heat.

For many nights he had a dream of walking to a black spot in the ice, poking through the remnants with a pitchfork, how the silver bridle ornaments still glistened somehow. He could hear the sound of hooves, which sounded like ice breaking up. Now, every spring, when he drifts over that spot where they did the burning, he looks down over the edge of the boat and imagines the bones resting on the bottom, the horse in full gallop, her breath streaming out like clouds of snow underwater.

Richard Brautigan

CORPORAL

Once I had visions of being a general. This was in Tacoma during the early years of World War II when I was a child going to grade school. They had a huge paper drive that was brilliantly put together like a military career.

It was very exciting and went something like this: If you brought in fifty pounds of paper you became a private and seventy-five pounds of paper were worth a corporal's stripes and a hundred pounds to be a sergeant, then spiraling pounds of paper leading upward until finally you arrived at being a general.

I think it took a ton of paper to be a general or maybe it was only a thousand pounds. I can't remember the exact amount but in the beginning it seemed so simple to gather enough paper to be a general.

I started out by gathering all the loose paper that was lying innocently around the house. That added up to three or four pounds. I'll have to admit that I was a little disappointed. I don't know where I got the idea that the house was just filled with paper. I actually thought there was paper all over the place. It's an interesting surprise that paper can be deceptive.

I didn't let it throw me, though. I marshaled my energies and went out and started going door to door asking people if they had any newspapers or magazines lying around that could be donated to the paper drive, so that we could win the war and destroy evil forever.

An old woman listened patiently to my spiel and then she gave me a copy of *Life* magazine that she had just finished reading. She closed the door while I was still standing there staring dumbfoundedly at the magazine in my hands. The magazine was warm.

At the next house, there wasn't any paper, not even a used envelope, because another kid had already beaten me to it.

At the next house, nobody was home.

That's how it went for a week, door after door, house after house, block after block, until finally I got enough paper together to become a private.

I took my goddamn little private's stripe home in the absolute bottom of my pocket. There were already some paper officers, lieutenants and captains, on the block. I didn't even bother to have the stripe sewed on my coat. I just threw it in a drawer and covered it up with some socks.

I spent the next few days cynically looking for paper and lucked into a medium pile of *Collier's* from somebody's basement, which was enough to get my corporal's stripes that immediately joined my private's stripe under the socks.

The kids who wore the best clothes and had a lot of spending money and got to eat hot lunch every day were already generals. They had known where there were a lot of magazines and their parents had cars. They strutted military airs around the playground and on their way home from school.

Shortly after that, like the next day, I brought a halt to my glorious military career and entered into the disenchanted paper shadows of America where failure is a bounced check or a bad report card or a letter ending a love affair and all the words that hurt people when they read them.

Gregory Burnham

SUBTOTALS

Number of refrigerators I've lived with: 18. Number of rotten eggs I've thrown: 1. Number of finger rings I've owned: 3. Number of broken bones: 0. Number of Purple Hearts: 0. Number of times unfaithful to wife: 2. Number of holes in one, big golf: 0; miniature golf: 3. Number of consecutive push-ups, maximum: 25. Number of waist size: 32. Number of gray hairs: 4. Number of children: 4. Number of suits, business: 2; swimming: 22. Number of cigarettes smoked: 83. Number of times I've kicked a dog: 6. Number of times caught in the act, any act: 64. Number of postcards sent: 831; received: 416. Number of spider plants that died while under my care: 34. Number of blind dates: 2. Number of jumping jacks: 982,316. Number of headaches: 184. Number of kisses, given: 21,602; received: 20,041. Number of belts: 21. Number of fuckups, bad: 6; not so bad: 1,500. Number of times swore under breath at parents: 838. Number of weeks at church camp: 1. Number of houses owned: 0. Number of houses rented: 12. Number of hunches played: 1,091. Number of compliments, given: 4,051; accepted: 2,249. Number of embarrassing moments: 2,258. Number of states visited: 38. Number of traffic tickets: 3. Number of girlfriends: 4. Number of times fallen off playground equipment, swings: 3; monkey bars: 2; teeter-totter: 1. Number of times flown in dreams: 28. Number of times fallen down stairs: 9. Number of dogs: 1. Number of cats: 7. Number of miracles witnessed: 0. Number of insults, given: 10,038; received: 8,963. Number of wrong telephone numbers dialed: 73. Number of times speechless: 33. Number of times stuck key into electrical socket: 1. Number of birds killed with rocks: 1. Number of times had the wind knocked out of me: 12. Number of times patted on the back: 181. Number of times wished I was dead: 2. Number of times unsure of footing: 458. Number of times fallen asleep reading a book: 513. Number of times born again: 0. Number of times seen double: 28. Number of déjà vu experiences: 43. Number of emotional breakdowns: 1. Number of times choked on bones, chicken: 4; fish: 6; other: 3. Number of times didn't believe parents: 23,978. Number of lawn-mowing miles: 3,575. Number of light bulbs changed: 273. Number of childhood home telephone: 384-621-5844. Number of brothers: 3½. Number of passes at women: 5. Number of stairs walked, up: 745,821; down: 743,609. Number of hats lost: 9. Number of magazine subscriptions: 41. Number of times seasick: 1. Number of bloody noses: 16. Number of times had sexual intercourse: 4,013. Number of fish caught: 1. Number of times heard "The Star Spangled Banner": 2,410. Number of babies held in arms: 9. Number of times I forgot what I was going to say: 631.

Gary Gildner

FINGERS

When Ronald, Mr. Lacey's son, came home from the war, he showered, put on a pair of new jeans and a new T-shirt, found his old high-school baseball cap and pulled it down snug over his forehead, then went outside and shot baskets. He shot baskets for about two weeks. One day Mr. Lacey said, "What about that money you saved up? What are you going to do with it?" Ronald shot baskets for a while longer, then went downtown and bought an old Hudson Hornet. He spent five days driving the Hudson back and forth through town, stopping for a root beer when he got thirsty. On the sixth day, when a tire went flat, Ronald locked the car and put his thumb in the air. The next day in the Atkins Museum in Kansas City, he bought a dozen picture postcards of Houdon's bust of Benjamin Franklin, because with that bald top and that long hair in back that fell to his shoulders, Franklin looked like the queerest duck he'd ever seen. Also Franklin seemed peeved about something. Then Ronald took a bus to New York City. The ride was nothing to crow about—and for maybe three hundred miles a man next to him wanted to describe losing his prostate gland. In New York, Ronald found a room a stone's throw from Yankee Stadium. He sent one of the Franklin cards to his father, saying only "Love, Ronald." Then he sat looking out the window. On the fire escape was a piece of red balloon that the wind was trying to blow away. Finally the wind succeeded and Ronald was tired. He took off his clothes, climbed into bed, and began to count the fingers on his shooting hand.

Jo Sapp

NADINE AT 35: A SYNOPSIS

The brain cells slip away, one by one by one. One hundred thousand of them a day, departing. If she is very still and concentrates very hard she can feel it happen. One by one by one, the cells descending to her rump. It is an exodus, a relocation. A mass conservation. Her brain is escaping.

And so, she discovers, is her husband.

"All I need is a little time," he says, his brown eyes wet and earnest as a cocker spaniel's. "Kind of a vacation from marriage. A year or two to find myself."

And she didn't even know he was lost.

She bounces back quickly. "So go," she says. "What the hell," her vocabulary impoverished already by virtue of the missing cells. She figures she has lost over twelve billion to date, and counting, but is uneasy about numbers, so might be wrong.

"What the hell," she says again, and helps him pack.

In retrospect she realizes that his defection might be related in cause to her word loss. He, too, is over thirty-five, and has, in fact, been losing cells for six months longer than she. His, at least, did not settle in his rump. She wonders exactly where they went, but cannot summon the energy to look for them. And she cannot ask him, for by the time she thinks of it he is halfway to California.

She sells the house and buys a car, gets a haircut, and prowls the bars. When she has the time. She cannot search for herself because, unlike her husband, she has yet to fully realize that she is lost. She would like to return to school, to become a nuclear engineer, or perhaps a dietitian. There is, however, a problem. Only two worn suits, a set of golf clubs, three monogrammed neckties, and a few billion brain cells were left behind by the vacating husband. The money he took.

So here she is, brain cells oozing out, slipping southward, with three children, a dog, two cats, and a goldfish. Hungry mouths. She does what any other right-thinking thirty-five-year-old American girl would do. She gets a job, subscribes to *Ms.*, deletes the word *girl*, along with *housewife* and *mankind*, from her vocabulary, further limiting it, and decides to take a lover. As for the children, she has an extra key to the apartment made for each of them and tells them to fend for themselves. That is the American way.

Finding a lover is difficult. Lovers for thirty-five-year-old brain-diminished vocabulary-impoverished women are in short supply. Particularly for those with three children and miscellaneous pets, even if they do all fend for themselves. So she resigns herself to celibacy, broken by occasional chance encounters and bouts of masturbation. It is a not altogether satisfactory life, but it has its rewards.

She finds, to her surprise, that she enjoys working, and is good at her job. She is a teller at a savings and loan. So friendly is she, so helpful, and so accurate in tabulating the amount of money in her drawer at day's end—never having to add a penny secretly or take away two—that in time she is promoted to New Accounts. She will go far, they tell her, and she knows they are right.

She makes more money now, and hires a housekeeper. The children and pets are fended for.

She controls the numbers of her life.

The second vice-president of the S&L invites her to dinner.

She accepts.

She is promoted to Business Loans.

The brain cells still escape, but she has no time to notice.

She has found herself without really looking.

And then one day the dog eats the goldfish and the cats get distemper. Her older boy steals a lace bra and the girl gets the measles. The younger boy sulks. The sink backs up in the bathroom and the housekeeper quits. She finds twelve gray hairs at her left temple and her life insurance lapses. Her husband always handled that sort of thing.

The second vice-president's wife calls her a name that she wishes had been deleted from her vocabulary, and she realizes she is no longer thirty-five. Then her husband telephones from Oregon where he has been working on a lumber crew and drinking beer and sleeping around since he left California and tells her he is tired of his vacation and wants to come home. She feels the cells slipping, and her rump widens alarmingly.

"What the hell," she says.

Roland Topor

FEEDING
THE HUNGRY

Y‌ou're bound to think I'm a liar: but I've never felt hungry. I don't know what hunger means. As far back as I can remember I've never known what it was like. I eat, of course, but without appetite. I feel absolutely nothing, not even distaste. I just eat.

People often ask me, "How do you manage to eat, then?" I have to admit that I don't know. What happens usually is that I'm sitting at a table and there's a plateful of food in front of me.

Since I'm rather absentminded I very soon forget about it. When I think about it again, the plate is empty. That's what happens.

Does this mean that I eat under hypnosis, in some kind of dissociated state? Certainly not. I said that this is what usually happens. But not always. Sometimes I remember the plate of food in front of me. But that doesn't stop me from emptying it all the same.

Naturally I've tried fasting. But that didn't work. I got thinner and thinner. I gave up just in time. A little longer and I would have died of hunger without knowing it. This experience frightened me so much that I now eat all the time. That way I don't worry. I'm tall and strong, and I have to keep the machine going. For other people, hunger provides a warning; since I am deprived of it I have to be doubly careful. As I said earlier, I'm absentminded. To forget would be fatal. I prefer to eat all the time: it's safer. I realize too that when I don't eat I become nervous and irritable, and don't know what to do about it. Instead, I smoke too much and drink too much, which is bad.

In the street I am frequently accosted by gaunt men dressed in rags. They gaze at me with fever-bright eyes and stammer out, "We're hungry!" I look at them with hatred. They eat only a crust of dry bread once a month, if that, but they enjoy it. "Hungry, are you!" I say to them nastily. "You're lucky."

Sobs rattle in their throats. Shudders rack them. Eventually they move off with slow, hesitant steps. As for me, I go into the first restaurant I see. Will the miracle occur? My heart beats fast as I swallow the first mouthful. A terrible despair overwhelms me. Nothing. Nothing at all. No appetite. I take my revenge by eating furiously, like someone drowning their sorrow in drink.

I leave the restaurant weighed down with food and hatred. For

I'm becoming bitter. I'm beginning to detest other people, people who are hungry. I hate them. So they're hungry, are they? I hope they die of hunger! I shan't be sorry for them! After all, thinking about people who are hungry while I'm eating is the only pleasure left to me.

Translated by Margaret Crosland and David LeVay

Michael Martone

DISH NIGHT

Every Wednesday night was Dish Night at the Wells Theatre. And it worked because she was there, week in and week out. She sat through the movie to get her white bone china. A saucer. A cup. The ushers stood on chairs by the doors and reached into the big wooden crates. There was straw all over the floor of the lobby and balls of newspaper from strange cities. I knew she was the girl for me. I'd walk her home. She'd hug the dish to her chest. The street lights would be on and the moon behind the trees. She'd talk about collecting enough pieces for our family of eight. "Oh, it's everyday and I know it," she'd say, holding it at arm's length. "They're so modern and simple and something we'll have a long time after we forget the movies."

I forget just what happened then. We heard about Pearl Harbor at a Sunday matinee. They stopped the movie, and a man came out on stage. The blue stage lights flooded the gold curtain. It was dark in there, but outside it was bright and cold. They didn't finish the show. Business would pick up then, and the Wells Theatre wouldn't need a Dish Night to bring the people in. The one we had gone to the week before was the last one ever, and we hadn't known it. The gravy boat looked like a slipper. I went to the war, to Europe where she'd write to me on lined school paper and never failed to mention we were a few pieces shy of the full set.

This would be the movie of my life, this walking home under the moon from a movie with a girl holding a dinner plate under her arm like a book. I believed this is what I was fighting for. Everywhere in Europe I saw broken pieces of crockery. In the farmhouses, the cafes. Along the roads were drifts of smashed china. On a beach, in the sand where I was crawling, I found a bit of it the sea washed in, all smooth with blue veins of a pattern.

I came home and washed the dishes every night, and she stacked them away, bowls nesting in bowls as if we were moving the next day.

The green field is covered with these tables. The sky is huge and spread with clouds. The pickup trucks and wagons are backed in close to each table so that people can sit on the lowered tailgates. On the tables are thousands of dishes. She walks ahead of me. Picks up a cup then sets it down again. A plate. She runs her finger along a rim. The green field rises slightly as we walk, all the places set at the tables. She hopes she will find someone else who saw the movies she saw on Dish Night. The theater was filled with people. I was there. We do this every Sunday after church.

GRACE PERIOD

You notice first a difference in the quality of space. The sunlight is still golden through the dust hanging in the drive-way, where your wife pulled out a few minutes ago in the Celica on a run to the mailbox, and the sky is still a regular blue, but it feels as if for an instant everything stretched just slightly, a few millimeters, then contracted again.

You shut off the electric hedge trimmers, thinking maybe vibration is affecting your inner ear. Then you are aware that the dog is whining from under the porch. On the other hand you don't hear a single bird song. A semi shifts down with a long backrap of exhaust on the state highway a quarter mile away. A few inches above one horizon an invisible jet is drawing a thin white line across the sky.

You are about to turn the trimmers on again when you have the startling sense that the earth under your feet has taken on a charge. It is not quite a trembling, but something like the deep throb of a very large dynamo at a great distance. Simultaneously there is a fluctuation of light, a tiny pulse, coming from behind the hills. In a moment another, and then another. Again and more strongly you have the absurd sense that everything inflates for a moment, then shrinks.

Your heart strikes you in the chest then, and you think instantly *aneurysm!* You are 135 over 80, and should have had a checkup two months ago. But no, the dog is howling now, and he's not alone. The neighbors' black lab is also in full cry, and in the distance a dozen others have begun yammering.

You stride into the house, not hurrying but not dawdling either, and punch in the number of a friend who lives in the city on the other side of the hills, the county seat. After the tone dance a long pause, then a busy signal. You consider for a moment, then dial the local volunteer fire chief, whom you know. Also busy.

Stretching the twenty-foot cord, you peer out the window. This time the pulse is unmistakable, a definite brightening of the sky to the west, and along with it a timber somewhere in the house creaks. You punch the Sheriff. Busy. Highway Patrol. Busy. 911. Busy. A recorded voice erupts, strident and edged with static, telling you all circuits are busy.

You look outside again and now there is a faint shimmering in the air. On the windowsill outside, against the glass, a few flakes of ash have settled. KVTX. Busy. The *Courier*. Busy. On some inexplicable frantic whim you dial out of state, to your father-in-law (Where is your wife, she should have the mail by now?), who happens to be a professor of geology on a distinguished faculty. The ringing signal this time. Once. Twice. Three times. A click.

"Physical plant."

Doctor Abendsachs, you babble, you wanted Doctor Abendsachs.

"This is physical plant, buddy. We can't connect you here."

What's going on, you shout, what is happening with the atmosphere—

He doesn't know. They are in a windowless basement. Everything fine there. It's lunchtime and they are making up the weekly football pool.

It is snowing lightly now outside, on the driveway and lawn and garage. You can see your clippers propped pathetically against the hedge. Once more, at top speed, you punch your father-in-law's number. Again a ringing. A click.

This time a recording tells you that all operators are busy and your call will be answered by the first available. The voice track ends and a burst of music begins. It is a large studio orchestra, heavy on violins, playing a version of "Hard Day's Night." At the point where the lyrics would be "sleeping like a log" the sound skips, wobbles, and skips again as if an old-fashioned needle has been bumped from a record groove.

You look out the window once more, as the house begins to shudder, and see that it is growing brighter and brighter and brighter.

Mary Morris

THE HAIRCUT

I knew the moment he got on the plane that something wasn't right, but what it was eluded me. He stood there in his khaki suit, tennis racket in hand, his teenage boys beaming on either side. I stood, our daughter in my arms, flanked by my parents. We faced one another the way I'd seen the British and French do in old Revolutionary War films.

What is wrong with this picture? I asked myself, recalling a test I'd often failed as a child. I was gullible, good at believing. (The dog belonged eating at the table; the wife could wear her husband's hat.) I knew everyone was expecting me to greet this man from whom I'd been estranged, for this was our time of reconciliation, the time to make up for what had been. We had reached this decision together after living apart and on opposite coasts for a year.

We had been estranged since before the child was born. He couldn't handle the additional responsibility; I clung more than I should. I had wanted a family; he still struggled to get beyond the one he already had. We had tried to separate and failed. I took a job in California, where I moved with my small child. He stayed on the East Coast. But we spoke every day on the phone. Each of us made several trips back and forth. I agreed to leave my West Coast job. He said he would try again.

Two months had passed since we had seen each other. I still felt annoyed with him for breaking our Valentine's plans (a ski trip he'd promised the boys came up). I had gotten miffed over his not calling when he said he would. I hurt over disappointments, large and small, but now I had come with our daughter to my parents' house in Florida, and he had come with the boys. It was to be a family vacation, our time to reconcile.

Look again, I told myself, still unable to decide what bothered me, what seemed wrong. His face looked handsome, almost tanned. His suit was neat and pressed. His eyes were clear and bright, his shoes polished. His beard and hair were neat and trimmed.

I paused there. For if you spend five years of your life with someone, you pay attention to certain things. This is a man of quirks, little oddities you don't forget. He won't eat oatmeal if it has any lumps. He won't wear a watch. When hurt, he recoils. He must play tennis every day. He has a way he hunches when he's telling an untruth. And he won't walk into a barbershop. In fact he prides himself in not having been in a barbershop in twenty-five years. I had cut his hair for the past five; his ex-wife had done the same for innumerable years before that. This man was a willing Samson to his Delilahs. Two months had passed since I'd seen him, yet his hair was neat and trim.

It felt as if the meaning of a dream were suddenly revealed, as if a foreign code had been cracked. The broken Valentine's weekend, the missed phone calls, the colleague he always needed to see. Suddenly in one lucid moment, standing there in the airport, my family by my side, his next to him, all of us happy to be in a place where it was sunny and warm, the pieces of the puzzle fit together as I had been trying to get them to for so long.

It was a crystallizing, a coming together, an epiphany, if you will, as if a fog had lifted. I had no more doubt. Nothing was unsure. As he stepped forward to embrace me, I said, "Who cut your hair?" He stepped back, but I held my ground. "Tell me," I said, moving our child to my shoulder, "Who cut your hair?"

Kenneth Bernard

VINES

Lately I notice that I *smell* more. I used to be able to wear the same shirt three or four days without being aware of it. Now, even in the course of a day, it smells foul. *I* smell foul. It doesn't seem to matter whether or not I take cosmetic precaution. My *deodorants* smell foul by the end of the day. Along with this my feet are getting colder and sweating differently. My blood is circulating less. I think about my teeth a lot. Not too long ago I used to begin days feeling on top of things. Lately I realize I'm full of little stratagems to hold it all together. I wiggle a toe here, take an extra breath there, tighten my buttocks inconspicuously on the subway. I asked my wife recently whether or not she ever got that rotten fruit feeling, that sense of galloping inner deterioration before falling from the vine with a sickening *plush*. She answered quickly and emphatically, as befits a Vassar girl: "No," she said, "I don't. I get tired. I get headaches. I get disgusted. And I get periods." There was a pause. "*Sometimes*," I said, repaying her for the speed and emphasis of her answer. She cackled. All things considered, she wasn't bad.

Not so my friend Norman. "What do you mean, that rotten fruit feeling?" he said. Norman is a health culturist. He does a lot of yoga and eats well. He impresses people as having a clean system. "Look," he said. "Maybe *you've* got to go, but *I* don't." I wondered whether he had moved on to something besides yoga. "I've told you for years," he said, "that you are literally full of rotten shit." I don't really like talking to Norman. For one thing, he never knows what I'm talking about. But my wife and his went to elementary school together. I'm really waiting for him to get a hernia before I talk to him seriously. I have several friends like Norman.

It actually comes down to the fact that I can talk to my wife best of all. Not that I don't make her sick a lot. But we've been together twenty-five years. That kind of thing is stronger than just about anything. Who else, for example, knows how many inconsequential and humiliating things my body has been through? "Look," she said, "the fact is that you're going to die sooner or later. Some bodies are in better shape for it than others." It was a devastating statement in its ambiguity. "You know," I said, "Norman isn't really so dumb. What kind of shape is Marie in?" Marie is Norman's wife. "Do you really want to know?" she said. "Well, yes. Why not?" "She thinks she might have cancer. She's having a biopsy Tuesday." "My God," I said.

My wife has a way of shortening my conversations. It's not just that she's a busy and successful woman. Through inadvertence or intent she frequently misconstrues my words just to that extent that I cannot respond to what she says. I am very subtly confused. I used to consider it girlish charm, but I don't anymore. It rather upsets me. I met Norman later in the week of his wife's biopsy. He practically hugged me. "Listen," he said, "why don't you start working out?" He looked at me with a lot of pain in his eyes, as if it was really important. "Norman, I'm really in a hurry," I said, moving off. "We'll talk about it." From half a block he shouted: "She's all right! She's all right!" It was all I could do not to run.

Two days later, for reasons totally beyond me, I felt like a heart-to-heart talk with my wife. *Her* name is Edna. "Listen," I began auspiciously, "I realize we're *both* going to die." She stared at me. "And I want you to know it's all right." Her mouth opened, but she didn't speak. "I mean, the children, the twenty-five, or thirty, or . . . years, I mean, let me say something ridiculous . . . I just want you to know that I love you." Having spoken with my usual clarity, I was about to speak again. But she forestalled me. "Will you please *shut up*," she hissed. Her eyes filled with tears. She gripped my hand, tightly, lovingly. *Lovingly.* That's rather important in retrospect. *"Will you please shut up!"* I did.

Rod Kessler

HOW TO TOUCH A BLEEDING DOG

It begins as nothing, as a blank. A rose light is filtering through the curtains. Rosy and cozy. My blanket is green. My blanket is warm. I am inside. Inside is warm. Outside is the dawn. Outside is cold. Cold day. My arm reaches for a wife who is no longer there.

The stillness is broken by the voice of a neighbor, yelling from the road outside. "The dog! Your dog's been hit!" It's the farmer down the road, keeping farmer's hours. "The dog!"

It's not my dog, but it is my responsibility. It is Beth's dog. I don't even like him, with his nervous habit of soiling the kitchen floor at night. I used to clean up after the dog before Beth came yawning out of our bed, and that was an act of love, but not of the dog. Now it doesn't matter why I clean up. Or whether.

Beth's dog is old and worn. He smells like a man given to thin cigars. Beth found him at the animal shelter, the oldest dog there.

I find the dog quivering on his side where he limped from the road. He has come to the garden gate, where the rose bushes bloom. A wound on his leg goes cleanly to the bone, and red stains appear here and there on the dull rug of his coat. He will not stand or budge when I coax him. A thick brown soup flows out of his mouth onto the dirt.

On the telephone, the veterinarian asks me what he looks like, and I say, stupidly, like an old Airedale. He means his wounds. After I describe them, he instructs me to wrap the dog in something warm and rush him over.

I make a mitten of the green blanket and scoop up the dog. The thought of touching his gore puts me off, and I am clumsy. I scoop weeds and clods as well as the dog. The dew on the grass looks cool, but the blood that blossoms on the blanket is warm and sick. He is heavy in my arms and settles without resistance in my car. He is now gravity's dog.

Driving past the unplowed fields toward town, I wonder if my clumsiness hurt the dog. Would Beth have touched him? The oldest dog in the shelter! It's a wonder that she thought having a dog would help.

The veterinarian helps me bring the dog from the car to the office. We make a sling of the blanket, I at the head. We lay him out on a steel-topped table. I pick weeds and grass from the blanket and don't know what to say.

The veterinarian clears his throat but then says nothing.

"He's my wife's dog," I say. "Actually, he came from the shelter over on High Street. He wasn't working out, really. I was thinking of returning him."

The veterinarian touches a spot below the dog's eye.

"Maybe," I continue, "maybe if it's going to cost a lot . . ."

"I don't think you have to make that decision," says the veterinarian, who points out that some pupillary response is missing. "He's dying," he says. "It's good you weren't attached to him."

Beth, I remembered, enjoyed taking the dog for rides in the car.

"These breaths," the veterinarian is saying, "are probably his last."

He seems relieved that he needn't bother to act appropriately for the sake of any grief on my part. He asks, "Did he run in the road a lot?"

"Never," I say. "He never ran at all."

"What do you make of that?"

"Beats me," I say, lying. I watch the dog's chest rise and fall. He's already far away and alone. I picture myself running out into the road.

I watch my hand volunteer itself and run its fingers through the nap of his head, which is surprisingly soft. And, with my touch on him, he is suddenly dead.

I walk back to the car and am surprised by how early in the day it still is. Blood is drying on the green blanket in my hand, but it will come off in the wash. The blood on the carpet of the car is out of sight, and I will pretend it isn't there. And then there's the touch. But soon the touch, too, will be gone.

GIRL

Wash the white clothes on Monday and put them on the stone heap; wash the color clothes on Tuesday and put them on the clothesline to dry; don't walk barehead in the hot sun; cook pumpkin fritters in very hot sweet oil; soak your little cloths right after you take them off; when buying cotton to make yourself a nice blouse, be sure that it doesn't have gum on it, because that way it won't hold up well after a wash; soak salt fish overnight before you cook it; is it true that you sing benna in Sunday school?; always eat your food in such a way that it won't turn someone else's stomach; on Sundays try to walk like a lady and not like the slut you are so bent on becoming; don't sing benna in Sunday school; you mustn't speak to wharf-rat boys, not even to give directions; don't eat fruits on the street—flies will follow you; *but I don't sing benna on Sundays at all and never in Sunday school;* this is how to sew on a button; this is how to make a buttonhole for the button you have just sewed on; this is how to hem a dress when you see the hem coming down and so to prevent yourself from looking like the slut I know you are so bent on becoming; this is how you iron your father's khaki shirt so that it doesn't have a crease; this is how you iron your father's khaki pants so that they don't have a crease; this is how you grow okra—far from the house, because okra tree harbors red ants; when you are growing dasheen, make sure it gets plenty of water or else it makes your throat itch when you are eating it; this is how you sweep a corner; this is how you sweep a whole house; this is how you sweep a yard; this is how you smile to someone you don't like very much; this is how you smile to someone you don't like at all; this is how you smile to someone you like completely; this is how you set a table for tea; this is how you set a table for dinner; this is how you set a table for dinner with an important guest; this is how you set a table for lunch; this is how you set a table for breakfast; this is how to behave in the presence of men who don't know you very well, and this way they won't recognize immediately the slut I have warned you against becoming; be sure to wash every day, even if it is with your own spit; don't squat down to play marbles—you are not a boy, you know; don't pick people's flowers—you might catch something; don't throw stones at blackbirds, because it might not be a blackbird at all; this is how to make a bread pudding; this is how to make doukona; this is how to make pepper pot; this is how to make a good medicine for a cold; this is how to make a good medicine to throw away a child before it even becomes a child; this is how to catch a fish; this is how to throw back a fish you don't like, and that way something bad won't fall on you; this is how to bully a man; this is how a man bullies you; this is how to love a man, and if this doesn't work there are other ways, and if they don't work don't feel too bad about giving up; this is how to spit up in the air if you feel like it, and this is how to move quick so that it doesn't fall on you; this is how to make ends meet; always squeeze bread to make sure it's fresh; *but what if the baker won't let me feel the bread?;* you mean to say that after all you are really going to be the kind of woman who the baker won't let near the bread?

Bruce Holland Rogers

THE BURLINGTON NORTHERN, SOUTHBOUND

Her name was Christine. He didn't know how to talk to her, so he wrote her a poem in which he compared her to the Burlington Northern southbound out of Fort Collins. He told her about the way he used to stand on the tracks in the dazzle of the headlight. He liked to step aside and stand on the tie edge to feel the thunder in his bones. Between the quaking of the cinders and his joy, the engine would almost bring him to his knees. The diesel throb in his guts would ebb until it was only sound, and then the cars—some shrieking on their springs—would *clataclat*

clataclat on by. He'd choose one car, and at a trot he would swing aboard the ladder. He'd feel the night air in his hair, and the cars nearest him would have a music all their own, a rhythm he could never hear if he only stood near the track as each one passed. The horn would sound for the last intersection, a song sweet as jazz. Then, from even fifty cars away, he would feel the vibration of the engine digging in. He would dream for a moment of hanging on, of riding the coupling platform through the night, riding for weary hours in a white-knuckled crouch until the daylight would show him the red hills of New Mexico and the smell of juniper would be in the air. Then he'd leave the dream to notice how fast the ties were flying beneath him. He'd lean out into the wind at the edge of town, and he'd launch himself into the void and land running with a jar he would feel all the way up his spine, a shock he would feel as a flash of white and the taste of electricity, and he'd run and run blindly and sometimes stumble in the cinders and scrape his knuckles and bang his knee. When he could stop at last he'd hear the blood rushing in his ears for a long time while he felt the train rush on and recede, and he'd watch the stars wheel awhile and when he walked home there'd be a ringing in his ears but gently.

He tried to put this in the poem. It was four pages long and ended:

> I want to ride you home, Christine,
> and beyond. I want to ride you into
> mornings sharp and cold and blue
> and never run the same track twice.

He never heard a word from her, not even to acknowledge that she had received the poem. What woman wants to hear she is like the Burlington Northern southbound?

Heinrich Böll

THE CAGE

A man stood beside the fence looking pensively through the barbed-wire thicket. He was searching for something human, but all he saw was this tangle, this horribly systematic tangle of wires—then some scarecrow figures staggering through the heat toward the latrines, bare ground and tents, more wire, more scarecrow figures, bare ground and tents stretching away to infinity. At some point there was said to be no more wire, but he couldn't believe it. Equally inhuman was the immmaculate, burning, impassive face of the blanched blue sky, where somewhere the sun floated just as pitilessly. The whole world was reduced to motionless scorching heat, held in like the breath of an animal under the spell of noon. The heat weighed on him like some appalling tower of naked fire that seemed to grow and grow and grow . . .

His eyes met nothing human; and behind him—he could see it more clearly, without turning round—was sheer horror. There they lay, those others, round the inviolable football field, packed side by side like rotting fish; next came the meticulously clean latrines, and somewhere a long way behind him was also paradise: the shady, empty tents, guarded by well-fed policemen . . .

How quiet it was, how hot!

He suddenly lowered his head, as if his neck were breaking under the fiery hammer-blow, and he saw something that delighted him: the delicate shadows of the barbed wire on the bare ground. They were like the fine tracery of intertwining branches, frail and beautiful, and it seemed to him that they must be infinitely cool, those delicate tracings, all linked with each other; yes, they seemed to be smiling, quietly and soothingly.

He bent down and carefully reached between the wires to pick one of the pretty branches; holding it up to his face he smiled, as if a fan had been gently waved in front of him. Then he reached out with both hands to gather up those sweet shadows. He looked left and right into the thicket, and the quiet happiness in his eyes faded: a wild surge of desire flared up, for there he saw innumerable little tracings which when gathered up must offer a precious, cool eternity of shadow. His pupils dilated as if about to burst out of the prison of his eyeballs: with a shrill cry he plunged into the thicket, and the more he became entangled in the pitiless little barbs the more wildly he flailed, like a fly in a spider's web, while with his hands he tried to grasp the exquisite shadow branches. His flailings were already stilled by the time the well-fed policemen arrived to free him with their wire-cutters.

Robert Hill Long

THE RESTRAINTS

Even when she was very little her hunger was worth something: hunger taught her to dance, and her father noticed. When his thirst was deep enough he could charm any bartender into clearing the narrow bar for just one dance—see, a girl, and feet so tiny. The patrons would shout for a second dance when they saw how the drumbeat of her bare feet could start such a trembling among the bottles on shelves. By the third or fourth dance, the trembling reached the glasses in their hands: they threw coins and bills at her feet to make her stop. Then her father would let her climb down and be a little girl again, mumbling thanks in poor English for the chair and spoon and bowls of stew brought her by drunken bricklayers and stevedores.

Afterwards, under the stars of whatever field they slept in, she'd dream the same dream: dancing in a dress with ruffles, polka dots. Some nights, still asleep, she'd rise and wander. Once she woke in the middle of a dirt road: an armadillo sniffed her, a train blew in the distance. Another time she woke on the porch of an old white couple. Her English was so poor they guessed she was deaf-mute. They bathed and fed her, aimed to adopt her. She was trying on a dress with blue dots in front of their radio full of Bing Crosby when her father knocked at the screen door. He made her choose between the dress and him. To protect his livelihood after that, he tied a rope from her ankle to his ankle at night. If she rose to leave, she fell.

It is many dances later, now, many dresses, many men later. The nurses who are otherwise kind tie her old-lady wrists down so she cannot rip out the IV again. Some nights her feet drum against the footboard, but weakly. When she can forget the re-straints, she goes over memories step by step: the time she was caught dancing in a bar at age ten and jailed for three days. Emerging, she saw her father at the corner holding his hat, which meant he was ashamed of himself. Out of his jacket he drew the most beautiful loaf of bread, which she ate before allowing him to kiss her. She remembers the night her stitched-up knee opened on stage in Chicago: with every spin she flung blood onto the front-row gowns and tuxedos. By then even her blood was famous.

But sometimes when she was ten, twelve, dancing in those bars, she would not stop. Not even after her father's guitar stopped.

She made the coins at her feet tremble and spin, kicked the sweaty
dollar bills back at the drinkers and shouters. Having the moment,
that was having everything. When she closes her eyes now she
knows who it is, tied to her on the narrow bed.

Ellen Hunnicutt

BLACKBERRIES

Just before noon the husband came down the near slope
of the hill carrying his cap filled with blackberries. "They're ripe
now. This week," he said to his wife. "We chose the right week
to come." He was a tall man, slender-limbed but thickening now
through the center of his body. He walked around the tent to
where the canvas water bag hung, spilled the berries into an
aluminum pan, and began to wash them gently.

"There isn't any milk left," his wife said. She was blond and
fragile, still pretty in a certain light and with a careful arrangement

of her features. "We finished the milk." She sat up from the blanket spread on the ground and laid aside the book she had been reading. "Albert and Mae went to New York," she said. "It's a tour. A theater tour."

"You told me that," he replied. "We can put these in cups. Cups will make fine berry bowls."

"There isn't any milk."

"I saw cattails," he said. "You'd think there would be too much woods for them. They need sun, but they're there. You can slice up cattail root and fry it. In butter. We have butter. It's good." He divided the berries into two cups and set one cup on the blanket beside his wife. He rummaged through the kitchen box and found a spoon, then began to eat his berries slowly and carefully, making them last.

"The tour covers everything," she said. "You only pay once. You pay one price."

"There aren't any bears here," he said, "nor dangerous snakes. It would be different if we were camped in a dangerous place. It's not like that here."

The woman smoothed the blanket she was sitting on with small, careful motions, as if making a bed. "It's going to be hot," she said. "There aren't any clouds, not even small ones."

"We can swim," he suggested, savoring his berries. "You always liked swimming. You're good at it."

"No, I'm not," she said. "I'm not good at it at all."

"You look great in a bathing suit. You always did. We have powdered milk."

"It has a funny taste."

"That green, silky bathing suit was the first one I ever saw you in."

"If we went down for milk we could go to the movie in the village. It's a musical. I looked when we drove through."

"They're probably only open on weekends," he said. "A little town like that. Powdered milk's okay."

"You don't like it at home. You told me you don't like powdered milk."

"I didn't say that," he replied. "Do you want me to go for the cattail root?"

"It's margarine," she said. "We have margarine, not butter."

"I'll fry them up."

"They're probably protected, like trillium."

"You can pick cattails," he said. "Nobody cares about cattails."

He went to the pile of fire logs and began splitting them, crouching, the hatchet working in clean, economical strokes. She watched him. He was good at splitting wood. The arc of arm and shoulder swung smoothly to aim each blow. "The summer's almost over," she said, taking one berry into her mouth. She mashed it with her tongue, chewed and swallowed. The sun passed its zenith and she saw a stripe of shadow appear on the grass beside her husband, a silhouette slim as a boy, tender as memory. She began to eat the berries in twos and threes, picking them out with her fingers, forgoing a spoon. "It's almost September." He turned to look at her. "No, it's not," he said. "It isn't, and it's scarcely noon. We have lots of time."

Julio Cortázar

A CONTINUITY
OF PARKS

He had begun to read the novel a few days before. He had put it down because of some urgent business conferences, opened it again on his way back to the estate by train; he permitted himself a slowly growing interest in the plot, in the characterizations. That afternoon, after writing a letter giving his power of attorney and discussing a matter of joint ownership with the manager of his estate, he returned to the book in the tranquillity of his study which looked out upon the park with its oaks. Sprawled in his favorite armchair, its back toward the door—even the possibility of an intrusion would have irritated him, had he thought of it—he let his left hand caress repeatedly the green velvet upholstery and set to reading the final chapters. He remembered effortlessly the names and his mental image of the characters; the novel spread its glamour over him almost at once. He tasted the almost perverse pleasure of disengaging himself line by line from the things around him, and at the same time feeling his head rest comfortably on the green velvet of the chair with its high back, sensing that the cigarettes rested within reach of his hand, that beyond the great windows the air of afternoon danced under the oak trees in the park. Word by word, caught up in the sordid dilemma of the hero and heroine, letting himself be absorbed to the point where the images settled down and took on color and movement, he was witness to the final encounter in the mountain cabin. The woman arrived first, apprehensive; now the lover came in, his face cut by the backlash of a branch. Admirably, she stanched the blood with her kisses, but he rebuffed her caresses, he had not come to perform again the ceremonies of a secret passion, protected by a world of dry leaves and furtive paths through the forest. The dagger warmed itself against his chest, and underneath liberty pounded, hidden close. A lustful, panting dialogue raced down the pages like a rivulet of snakes, and one felt it had all been decided from eternity. Even to those caresses which writhed about the lover's body, as though wishing to keep him there, to disuade him from it; they sketched abominably the frame of that other body it was necessary to destroy. Nothing had been forgotten: alibis, unforeseen hazards, possible mistakes. From this hour on, each instant had its use minutely assigned. The cold-blooded, twice-gone-over reexamination of the details was barely broken off so that a hand could caress a cheek. It was beginning to get dark.

Not looking at one another now, rigidly fixed upon the task

which awaited them, they separated at the cabin door. She was to follow the trail that led north. On the path leading in the opposite direction, he turned for a moment to watch her running, her hair loosened and flying. He ran in turn, crouching among the trees and hedges until, in the yellowish fog of dusk, he could distinguish the avenue of trees which led up to the house. The dogs were not supposed to bark, they did not bark. The estate manager would not be there at this hour, and he was not there. He went up the three porch steps and entered. The woman's words reached him over the thudding of blood in his ears: first a blue chamber, then a hall, then a carpeted stairway. At the top, two doors. No one in the first room, no one in the second. The door of the salon, and then, the knife in hand, the light from the great windows, the high back of an armchair covered in green velvet, the head of the man in the chair reading a novel.

Translated by Paul Blackburn

Michael Oppenheimer

THE PARING
KNIFE

I found a knife under the refrigerator while the woman I love and I were cleaning our house. It was a small paring knife that we lost many years before and had since forgotten about. I showed the knife to the woman I love and she said, "Oh. Where did you find it?" After I told her, she put the knife on the table and then went into the next room and continued to clean. While I cleaned the kitchen floor, I remembered something that happened four years before that explained how the knife had gotten under the refrigerator.

We had eaten a large dinner and had drunk many glasses of
wine. We turned all the lights out, took our clothing off, and
went to bed. We thought we would make love, but something
happened and we had an argument while making love. We had
never experienced such a thing. We both became extremely angry.
I said some very hurtful things to the woman I love. She kicked
at me in bed and I got out and went into the kitchen. I fumbled
for a chair and sat down. I wanted to rest my arms on the table
and then rest my head in my arms, but I felt the dirty dishes on
the table and they were in the way. I became incensed. I swept
everything that was on the table onto the floor. The noise was
tremendous, but then the room was very quiet and I suddenly felt
sad. I thought I had destroyed everything. I began to cry. The
woman I love came into the kitchen and asked if I was all right.
I said, "Yes." She turned the light on and we looked at the kitchen
floor. Nothing much was broken, but the floor was very messy.
We both laughed and then went back to bed and made love. The
next morning we cleaned up the mess, but obviously overlooked
the knife.

I was about to ask the woman I love if she remembered that
incident when she came in from the next room and without saying
a word, picked up the knife from the table and slid it back under
the refrigerator.

John Updike

THE WIDOW

Q: Nice place you have here.

A: I try to keep it up. But it's hard. It's hard.

Q: How many years has it been now?

A: Seven. Seven come September. He was sitting in that chair, right where you are now, and the next minute he was gone. Just a kind of long sigh, and he was gone.

Q: Sounds like a pretty good way to go. Since we all have to go sometime.

A: That's what everybody said. The minister, the undertaker. I suppose I should have been grateful, but if it had been less sudden, it might have been less of a shock. It was as if he *wanted* to go, the way he went so easy.

Q: Well. I doubt that. But it's you I'm interested in, you in the years since. You look wonderfully well.

A: Ever since I stopped taking the pills. These doctors nowadays, they prescribe the pills, I honestly believe, to kill you. I was having dizzy spells, one leg seemed to be larger than the other, my hands felt like they were full of prickers . . . it all stopped, once I stopped taking the pills.

Q: And your . . . mental state?

A: If you mean do I still have all my buttons, you'll have to judge that for yourself. Oh, I'm forgetful, but then I always was. I know if I stand in the middle of the room long enough it'll come to me. It's like the sleeping. At first I used to panic, but now if I wake up at three in the morning I just accept it as what my body wants. Trust your body, is the moral of it all I suppose.

Q: By mental state I meant more grief, loneliness, sense of self, since . . . you became a widow.

A: Well, first, there's the space. No, first, there's the ghosts. Then there's the space.

Q: Ghosts?

A: Oh yes, right there. All the time. Talking to me, telling me to put one foot in front of the other, not to panic. Rattling the latches at night. As certain as you're sitting there. Many a time I've seen it rock by itself.

Q: Perhaps I should change chairs.

A: Oh no, sit right there. People do all the time.

Q: After the ghosts, space?

A: An amazing amount of it. Amazing. I never noticed the sky before. Seventy years on earth and I never looked at the sky.

Just yesterday, there were clouds in it with little downward points, like a mountain range upside down, or a kind of wet handwriting, it looked ever so weird, I can't describe it properly. And the trees. The way the trees are so patient, so *themselves*, gathering their substance out of air—it sounds silly, in words.

Q: So you would say then that since your husband's passing your life has taken a turn toward the mystical?

A: Not mystical, *practical*. The income tax, for instance. I do it all myself, federal and state. I never knew I had it in me to enjoy numbers. And people. I have friends, of all ages. Too many at times, I take the phone off the hook. I think what I meant about the space before, it's space you can arrange yourself, there's nobody pushing at you with *his* space, nobody to tell you you're crazy when you're weeding the peas at four in the morning and start singing.

Q: You often sing to yourself?

A: I'm not sure.

Q: I don't mean to pry—

A: Then don't pry.

One must be prepared, in interviewing the elderly, for these sudden changes of mood, for abrupt closure of access. Human material rubbed so thin by longevity resembles a book whose pages in their tissue fineness admit phrases from the next page or, in their long proximity *en face*, have become scrambled inky mirrors one of the other. Paranoia is the natural state of a skidding organism. Volatility is the inevitable condition of angels. The widow's face, so uncannily tranquil and spacious before, has grown hard and narrow as a gem that is cutting the transparent interface of the interview. One must return to scratch:

Q: But, er, ma'am, prying wasn't—I mean, what we want to do here, your testimony is so positive, so unexpectedly so, that we want to bring to the widest possible audience . . . uh, its great value in this era of widows, to all those others who find themselves alone.

A: You are not alone. You are not. Not.

Jim Heynen

WHAT HAPPENED DURING THE ICE STORM

One winter there was a freezing rain. How beautiful! people said when things outside started to shine with ice. But the freezing rain kept coming. Tree branches glistened like glass. Then broke like glass. Ice thickened on the windows until everything outside blurred. Farmers moved their livestock into the barns, and most animals were safe. But not the pheasants. Their eyes froze shut.

Some farmers went ice-skating down the gravel roads with clubs to harvest the pheasants that sat helplessly in the roadside ditches.

The boys went out into the freezing rain to find pheasants too. They saw dark spots along a fence. Pheasants, all right. Five or six of them. The boys slid their feet along slowly, trying not to break the ice that covered the snow. They slid up close to the pheasants. The pheasants pulled their heads down between their wings. They couldn't tell how easy it was to see them huddled there.

The boys stood still in the icy rain. Their breath came out in slow puffs of steam. The pheasants' breath came out in quick little white puffs. Some of them lifted their heads and turned them from side to side, but they were blindfolded with ice and didn't flush. The boys had not brought clubs, or sacks, or anything but themselves. They stood over the pheasants, turning their own heads, looking at each other, each expecting the other to do something. To pounce on a pheasant, or to yell Bang! Things around them were shining and dripping with icy rain. The barbed-wire fence. The fence posts. The broken stems of grass. Even the grass seeds. The grass seeds looked like little yolks inside gelatin whites. And the pheasants looked like unborn birds glazed in egg white. Ice was hardening on the boys' caps and coats. Soon they would be covered with ice too.

Then one of the boys said, Shh. He was taking off his coat, the thin layer of ice splintering in flakes as he pulled his arms from the sleeves. But the inside of the coat was dry and warm. He covered two of the crouching pheasants with his coat, rounding the back of it over them like a shell. The other boys did the same. They covered all the helpless pheasants. The small gray hens and the larger brown cocks. Now the boys felt the rain soaking through their shirts and freezing. They ran across the slippery fields, unsure of their footing, the ice clinging to their skin as they made their way toward the blurry lights of the house.

K. C. Frederick

TEDDY'S
CANARY

And Louise calls him down—she's screaming her head off because the pipe just blew totally and water's shooting out from under the sink and Bernie must think she's popped an artery or something and he's out of that bathtub like a goosed whale."

Everybody around the table in Teddy's rec room is looking at each other, trying to imagine that. "I can just see him," I say, "dripping wet, leaving a trail of water on the steps and you know

Bernie, with that major-league beer belly of his he must have looked like the Jell-O Monster and there's Louise pointing to that pipe and him huffing and puffing and then he yells to her to go to the basement and shut off the water and you can imagine him trying to get his big ass under the sink and try to stop the spray with his towel."

We're all seeing him, we're all laughing at this story we've heard a dozen times before. I'm trying to tell it the way Teddy used to. We know he'd have done it better but we don't care about that, we want it to be like it was last spring. And it's nice that Rita has invited us over.

Spider is already starting to lose control, his big horse's head is bobbing up and down and Petey has this look on his face like a contestant on a game show waiting for the next question he's certain he can answer and Billy and Squirrel have their hands on their beers and there's something in their eyes, not amusement really and not remembering either, but more a kind of listening to a song you're sure you know but you can't name and I go on about how that dog comes into the kitchen while Bernie's still got his head under the sink trying to stop the leak.

"Little Pepper gets right up next to him and all of a sudden he starts yapping. Bernie jumps real quick, he whacks his head on the cabinet, and *bam!* he's out cold. Just at that second Louise shuts off the water and she comes up the stairs yelling 'Bernie, Bernie, is it off up there?' and what does she see but him laying on the floor naked, his legs under the sink and she starts wailing, 'Oh, my God. Oh, my God.' "

Spider's shaking his head, his eyes are wet, and for some crazy reason I'm so happy that he's laughing. For a second I think it's really Teddy telling the story. "And then," I say, "that canary they used to have that she was trying to clean the cage when all this started, it comes flying into the kitchen all yellow, flapping its wings, singing like crazy." I've always wondered: if one of them was unconscious and the other one was hysterical, who could have been paying any attention to that bird. But that's how Teddy told it. "And that dog gets real quiet, it must be thinking the master's dead, and Louise is at the top of the basement steps crossing herself, saying 'Holy Mary, mother of God,' and she's looking at that big naked corpse laying in the puddle on the kitchen floor and she's thinking, I'm not ready to be a widow yet."

I glance out the window at the traffic passing by in the early darkness and I'm glad I'm in here where it's warm. How can it be fall already, I wonder, with winter in the air? By Christmas Rita wants to be out of the house, she wants to move back to that little town where her folks are, and I suppose someone else will be telling different stories here in Teddy's rec room.

Everyone around the table's looking at me, as if they're afraid I won't go on. I know Teddy would have added something real good about Louise, like she was promising God she'd make Bernie go to church if by some miracle he comes back from the dead, but I just tell about how she's on the phone shouting at the cops to please hurry, she thinks her husband had a heart attack. My voice runs a little fast on that part and everybody's eyes around the table flicker a little as if someone just came into the room and walked off with one of the pictures of the old softball teams that are on the wall but no one's going to say anything about it. Then I'm telling about the dog licking Bernie's face and all of a sudden he's shouting "Get that fucking animal off me, what the hell am I doing down here?" and Louise is kneeling on the wet kitchen floor saying "Thank you, God, thank you so much" and that bird's chirping away from on top of the refrigerator.

Now everybody's smiling and for a while it seems as if nothing has changed, like we're ready to go out to the field tomorrow and play softball: you can smell the beer and the cigarettes and the pizza, and we're happy. I take a swallow of my drink. It feels cool going down my throat, and over my glass I look at everyone. I want to believe all the rest of us are going to be around here for a long time.

Chuck Rosenthal

THE NICEST KID
IN THE
UNIVERSE

Franky Gorky was the nicest kid in the universe. He always listened to his parents. He shared his toys and candy with other children. Birds sat on his bedroom window in the mornings and waited for him to wake up before they started to sing. Wild animals came up to Franky Gorky and ate out of his hand. Every kid who ever lived on 24th Street heard of Franky Gorky because he was the nicest kid who ever lived.

But he wasn't the smartest kid.

For one thing he never noticed the moon.

Franky Gorky never noticed the moon till one night in December his parents took him outside on a cold night after a snowstorm just after the Feast of the Immaculate Conception and the anniversary of Pearl Harbor, the night Greta and Gary Gorky took him outside and pointed to the crescent in the sky. Franky Gorky thought it was a funny street light. "No," said his dad, Gary Gorky, "it's the moon."

Well Franky Gorky didn't know what to think about the moon, though he wished it was round, and every night after he got put to bed he went to his bedroom window where the birds waited for him to wake up in the morning and went out and looked at the moon, which, he started to notice, was actually getting bigger, in fact after a while it looked like it was really going to get round. Of course he was a good kid and he knew good kids often got what they wished for, but he'd heard enough fairy tales where people got what they wished for, like King Midas, and it ended up doing more harm than good, lucky for him nobody else seemed to notice that the moon was getting rounder. He wished he could talk to his grandmother who wouldn't tell his parents and always seemed to know about stuff. In fact as the moon got bigger and bigger and one night got so big and white he thought it would suck his bones and maybe the bones of the whole world, something Franky Gorky didn't want responsibility for, Franky Gorky remembered that usually you just didn't get one wish, you got three wishes, and Franky Gorky stared up at the ice death moon and wished it would go away and that he could see his grandmother.

Franky Gorky may have been the nicest kid in the universe but that didn't mean he always did the right thing, even he realized that, and by the time the moon was about half gone again and he started feeling good he figured out that what he should have wished for was that the moon would go back to normal, not that it would go away completely. Wishing that it would go away completely was a big blunder, especially since he'd used his third wish on getting to see his grandmother who he found out was coming to see the Gorkys on Christmas like she always did.

So it was a sad Christmas Eve for Franky Gorky when the moon went out. He could barely think about his Christmas toys, and instead of lying awake all night trying to keep from thinking about what he was going to get for Christmas by thinking about the baby Jesus and the Wise Men and how the world was to be saved from Original Sin, he kept going to the window and looking for the moon which he'd wiped out with the abuse of his wish, and now all he had left was his grandmother, Grandma Gorky, who was driving in from Buffalo like she did every Christmas, who would listen to him and know what to do.

And Franky Gorky was up like a dart on Christmas morning, waiting at the front window for his Grandma Gorky, and when she came he did the first bad thing of his life, he ran out of the house without permission and headed across the street where Grandma Gorky had parked because Christmas visitors all over the neighborhood had taken all the parking places on the Gorkys' side, slipped on the ice, and got rubbed out by a drunk driver.

That's what happens, said my father, when people take other people's parking places.

That's what happens, said my mother, when you don't look both ways.

What happens is, if you're the nicest kid in the whole universe, then you have to die.

This is what happens when you try to explain something.

Kelly Cherry

THE PARENTS

We bring our babies, blue-eyed babies, brown-eyed babies; we have come to watch the parade, the marching bands. Young women step high; batons fly, flash against the sky like lightning rods. Oh, spare the child, for next come the floats. See Mickey Duck! See Donald Mouse! Snow White rides in her pumpkin carriage, faster, faster, speeding toward marriage with the prince who will give her babies, blue-eyed babies, brown-eyed babies, like our own babies, who are—lost. Lost at the parade! Where are our babies, our babies? We are looking for them everywhere, frantically, everyone helping and shouting: Find the babies!—when suddenly we see them. No wonder no one could find them. They have grown three feet taller, sprouted whiskers or breasts, swapped spun sugar for Sony Walkmen. We kiss them and hug them, but we are secretly frightened by their remarkable new size. They tell us not to worry. They will take care of us. And sure enough, later, we let them drive us home, because their eyes are sharper, their hands are steadier, and they know the way, which we forget more and more often. They stroke our hair and tell us to be calm. On Saturday, our babies help us to choose the best coffin. They are embarrassed when we insist on taking it home to try it out, but they give in because they don't want to upset us. After they leave for the cinema, we climb into the coffin and pull the lid over us. The salesman had said one wouldn't be big enough, then said one would not be sanitary. We laughed: Age has shrunk us. We are small enough to fit in here quite comfortably. It is as dark as a movie house, the kind in which we used to neck in the back row. Now, of course, nothing is playing. The film has completely unwound, and the only sound is the flicking of the loose end, around and around.

Fred Leebron

WATER

She touches his hair by the river.

I am in our apartment, working. Her hand moves down his back.

I empty the trash and unclog the kitchen sink. His former girlfriends have turned into lesbians.

I take the key to his apartment, which he gave me so I could water his plants during the summer. He bends his kissing face to hers.

I walk over to his apartment, just two blocks away. Their legs dangle in the river.

I unlock the door and bolt it behind me. The room smells of feet and stale ashtrays. In the kitchen is a gas stove. I turn it on without lighting it.

Down by the river is a flock of geese, which they admire while holding hands. Soon he will take her back to his apartment. Soon they will lie there, readying cigarettes.

I relock the apartment and slip into the street. The air smells of autumn, burnt. In the sky, birds are leading each other south.

I know there is nothing left between us, that she looks at me each morning as if I were interrupting her life.

STOCKINGS

.

Henry Dobbins was a good man, and a superb soldier, but sophistication was not his strong suit. The ironies went beyond him. In many ways he was like America itself, big and strong, full of good intentions, a roll of fat jiggling at his belly, slow of foot but always plodding along, always there when you needed him, a believer in the virtues of simplicity and directness and hard labor. Like his country, too, Dobbins was drawn toward sentimentality.

Even now, twenty years later, I can see him wrapping his girlfriend's pantyhose around his neck before heading out on ambush.

It was his one eccentricity. The pantyhose, he said, had the properties of a good-luck charm. He liked putting his nose into the nylon and breathing in the scent of his girlfriend's body; he liked the memories this inspired; he sometimes slept with the stockings up against his face, the way an infant sleeps with a magic blanket, secure and peaceful. More than anything, though, the stockings were a talisman for him. They kept him safe. They gave access to a spiritual world, where things were soft and intimate, a place where he might someday take his girlfriend to live. Like many of us in Vietnam, Dobbins felt the pull of superstition, and he believed firmly and absolutely in the protective power of the stockings. They were like body armor, he thought. Whenever we saddled up for a late-night ambush, putting on our helmets and flak jackets, Henry Dobbins would make a ritual out of arranging the nylons around his neck, carefully tying a knot, draping the two leg sections over his left shoulder. There were some jokes, of course, but we came to appreciate the mystery of it all. Dobbins was invulnerable. Never wounded, never a scratch. In August, he tripped a Bouncing Betty, which failed to detonate. And a week later he got caught in the open during a fierce little firefight, no cover at all, but he just slipped the pantyhose over his nose and breathed deep and let the magic do its work.

It turned us into a platoon of believers. You don't dispute facts.

But then, near the end of October, his girlfriend dumped him. It was a hard blow. Dobbins went quiet for a while, staring down at her letter, then after a time he took out the stockings and tied them around his neck as a comforter.

"No sweat," he said. "I still love her. The magic doesn't go away."

It was a relief for all of us.

Bernard Cooper

THE HURRICANE RIDE

In salt air and bright light, I watched my aunt revolve. Centrifugal force pressed her ample flesh against a padded wall. She screamed as the floor dropped slowly away, lipstick staining her teeth. But she stuck to the wall as if charged with static, and along with others, didn't fall. She was dressed in checks and dangling shoes, her black handbag clinging to her hip. The Hurricane Ride gathered speed. My aunt was hurtling, blurred. Her mouth became a long dark line. Her delirious eyes were multiplied.

Checks and flesh turned diaphanous, her plump arms, gartered thighs. Her face dissolved, a trace of rouge.

I swore I saw through her for the rest of the day, despite her bulk and constant chatter, to the sea heaving beyond the boardwalk, tide absconding with the sand, waves cooling the last of light. Even as we left, I saw the clam-shell ticket stand, the ornate seahorse gate, through the vast glass of my aunt.

When does speed exceed the ability of our eyes to arrest and believe? If the axial rotation of the earth is 1,038 miles per hour, why does our planet look languid from space, as bejeweled as my aunt's favorite brooch? Photographs of our galaxy, careening through the universe at over a million miles per hour, aren't even as blurred as the local bus.

Momentum. Inertia. Gravity. Numbers and theories barrel beyond me. It's clear that people disappear, and things, and thoughts. Earth. Aunt. Hurricane. Those words were written with the wish to keep them still. But they travel toward you at the speed of light. They are on the verge of vanishing.

William Brohaugh

A MOMENT
IN THE
SUN FIELD

Deep into the summer and not too long after Bobby Hansen's twelfth birthday, after one of Bobby's mom's hamburger suppers, Mike Pasqui came over to Bobby's house and the two of them talked Bobby's dad into playing some 500 with them. Dad grumbled a little—he always did—but he grabbed the bat and ball from the back porch and headed for the back yard with Mytzi, Bobby's muttzy dog, yapping behind—and he always did that, too.

Mike and Bobby took the field first, and Dad hit balls to them.

A caught fly ball earned Bobby 100 points. A grounder played on one bounce earned Mike 75. A flubbed grounder—a two-bouncer—stole 50 points back from Mike. And on it went into the evening. When one of the players earned 500 points, he took the bat until someone else got 500. Mike didn't do much batting, which was okay with him. He just liked being a part of the game. And since Dad preferred to bat, after a while he decided to do all the batting no matter who scored how many points. And that was okay with everyone, too.

Pretty soon, Bobby had 1,075 points, and Mike had around 300 (he had stopped counting), and Dad was swinging and smacking the ball and even joking around a little bit.

It wasn't too long and the shadow of the house slid up on Dad, slid over him, and stretched for the horizon, which it would reach, Bobby knew, the moment the sun disappeared below the opposite horizon. It would be a shadow hundreds of miles long, millions of miles long, and Bobby sometimes wondered if that was what night really was, all the shadows of all the houses and all the dads and all the kids playing 500 stretched out and added together.

Dad tossed the ball into the air in front of him and popped a fly out of the shadow and into the sunlight. The sun splashed onto one side of the ball, splashed it cool and white against the cool and darkening sky. The ball spun, and began to fall, and Bobby positioned himself under it, held his glove out not for a whole ball, but just a piece of one, because it looked like just a piece of one, a slice of ball, the slice splashed extra white in the high sunlight.

Bobby waited for that little bit of ball to come down, and suddenly he understood the moon.

Scott Russell Sanders

THE PHILOSOPHICAL COBBLER

The grandfather of General (later President) Ulysses S. Grant tanned hides and cobbled shoes in Pilgrim County. Neighbors knew him simply as Noah Grant, the close-tongued man to whom you took your skins for curing, from whom you bought your moccasins, or, if well-to-do, your boots.

For a long time no one expected him to become the father, let alone grandfather, of anybody. He was too sparing of words ever to put together a speech long enough to qualify as a marriage proposal. Contrary to the predictions of Roma's gossips, however, he did marry. In due time he fathered a son, Jesse, who fathered a son, Ulysses, who helped lead a multitude of other sons, both Union and Confederate, into premature graves.

Although he lived by tanning the hides of murdered animals, Noah did not like killing, and never fired a gun. Skins heaped all around him while he worked: bear, otter, marten, deer, the reeking wildcat and fox, panther and wolf, the sumptuous mink. The animal kingdom seemed to have shed its collective coat in his tanning shack. The longer he worked among hides, the more silent he became, as if the tannic acid were curing him of speech. Dumb beast among dumb beasts, the neighbors said.

In his silence, Noah never left off musing. Perhaps a way could be found to skin the animals without killing them, as sheep were sheared for their wool? Perhaps the deer and panthers could be bred so that each animal would bear a dozen thicknesses of skin, and thus fewer need be killed? Or maybe some vegetable could be trained to produce fur instead of fruit? Noah became, in short, a philosopher.

While his knife scraped fat from a raccoon skin, or his needle pierced the hide of an otter, he contemplated the world's secret equations: nine bearskins would buy you a rifle, forty-three would buy you a horse; between eighty-five and one hundred deer would get you a yoke of oxen; mink was worth about the same, inch per inch, as calico; for one muskrat you could get stinking drunk on rye whiskey, and for a panther you could stay that way a week. There was occult meaning in these equations. If you thought about them long enough, the grandfather of U. S. Grant was persuaded, you could deduce the paths of stars and the causes of war.

Sheila Barry

CORNERS

Mildred and Jessie were elected to inspect Marie's remains before the public viewing. Mildred got to go because she was the oldest, and Jessie because she had come the farthest. The other siblings had gotten to pick out the casket and the dress their sister, Marie, would wear.

The undertaker, a former high-school classmate, showed them solemnly into the parlor. "I think you'll be pleased," he said as he lifted the casket lid and stepped back.

Jessie felt a familiar tug of pity for him, like the one she'd feel when she'd encounter him in school the day after she and her sisters had been making fun of him the night before.

"She looks wonderful, Tom," Mildred said. "You've done a good job. What do you think, Jessie?"

Jessie was crying, sobbing from the shock of seeing Marie dead and hearing Mildred and Tom discussing her body as if it were a float they were preparing for the Fourth of July parade.

Mildred put an arm around her. "There, there, Jessie," she soothed. "We keep forgetting you weren't here for Marie's last year. If you had been, you'd understand. None of us want Marie dead but none of us wanted her to go on suffering."

"She doesn't have to be smiling," Jessie sobbed. She turned on Tom. "Why did you put that silly smile on her face?" she demanded.

Tom's face panicked. "You don't like it?" he asked. His eyes sought Mildred's for confirmation.

"If Jessie doesn't like it," Mildred said, "then I guess you'd better change it."

"What do you mean, change it?" Jessie asked. "You can't change something like that!"

Tom reached over. He took the index finger of his right hand and tugged down on one corner of Marie's mouth which responded as if it were made of soft, malleable clay. Tom stuck his finger in the other corner of Marie's mouth and tugged down again. He stepped back. "How's that?" he asked. "Is that better?"

Mildred looked at Jessie expectantly.

"We can do anything you want with the mouth, Jessie," Tom said. He poised his index finger. "You just tell me what you want."

Jessie fled. She ran out, past the parking lot, around the corner to the high-school playing field.

Mildred found her there, sitting on the grass, hugging her knees.

She sat down next to her. "Come on, kid," she said gently, "don't you think you're a little old for this?"

Jessie whipped her head around to look at Mildred. She thought she was ready, ready to tell Mildred what she really thought, how Mildred and Marie had been so close, how they had always left her out, even left her out of Marie's death. "Too old!" she demanded. "Too old?" she repeated to herself. That was the problem right there. None of them was any longer too young to die.

Mildred was smiling at her, tilting her head slightly to the side as if saying, Are you all right, are you ready to go on?

Jessie smiled back. Mildred nodded her head up and down, her smile growing with each movement. Then she poised her index finger in the air and waited.

Jessie laughed, quietly rocked back and forth, laughing until the tears rolled down her cheeks. She nodded and Mildred reached over with her index finger and pulled the corners of Jessie's mouth down. Jessie stuck out her index finger and pushed the corners of Mildred's mouth up. Down, up, down, up, they went, laughing then rolling on the ground until they could go back and tell Tom that Marie looked just fine.

Mark Strand

SPACE

A beautiful woman stood at the roof-edge of one of New York's tall midtown apartment houses. She was on the verge of jumping when a man, coming out on the roof to sunbathe, saw her. Surprised, the woman stepped back from the ledge. The man was about thirty or thirty-five and blond. He was lean, with a long upper body and short, thin legs. His black bathing suit shone like satin in the sun. He was no more than ten steps from the woman. She stared at him. The wind blew strands of her long dark hair across her face. She pulled them back and held them in place with one hand. Her white blouse and pale blue skirt kept billowing, but she paid no attention. He saw that she was barefoot and that two high-heeled shoes were placed side by side on the gravel near where she stood. She had turned away from him. The wind flattened her skirt against the front of her long thighs. He wished he could reach out and pull her toward him. The air shifted and drew her skirt tightly across her small, round buttocks; the lines of her bikini underpants showed. "I'll take you to dinner," he yelled. The woman turned to look at him again. Her gaze was point-blank. Her teeth were clenched. The man looked at her hands which were now crossed in front of her, holding her skirt in place. She wore no wedding band. "Let's go someplace and talk," he said. She took a deep breath and turned away. She lifted her arms as if she were preparing to dive. "Look," he said, "if it's me you're worried about, you have nothing to fear." He took the towel he was carrying over his shoulders and made it into a sarong. "I know it's depressing," he said. He was not sure what he had meant. He wondered if the woman felt anything. He liked the way her back curved into her buttocks. It struck him as simple and expressive; it suggested an appetite or potential for sex. He wished he could touch her. As if to give him some hope, the woman lowered her arms to her sides and shifted her weight. "I'll tell you what," the man said, "I'll marry you." The wind once again pulled the woman's skirt tightly across her buttocks. "We'll do it immediately," he said, "and then go to Italy. We'll go to Bologna, we'll eat great food. We'll walk around all day and drink grappa at night. We'll observe the world and we'll read the books we never had time for." The woman had not turned around or backed off from the ledge. Beyond her lay the industrial buildings of Long Island City, the endless row houses of Queens. A few clouds moved in the distance. The man shut his eyes and tried to think of how else to change her mind. When he opened them, he saw that between her feet and the ledge was a space, a space that would always exist now between herself and the world. In the long moment when she existed before him for the last time, he thought, How lovely. Then she was gone.

FEAR:
FOUR EXAMPLES

My daughter called from college. She is a good student, excellent grades, is gifted in any number of ways.

"What time is it?" she said. I said, "It is two o'clock." "All right," she said. "It's two now. Expect me at four—four by the clock that said it's two." "It was my watch," I said. "Good," she said.

It is ninety miles, an easy drive.

At a quarter to four, I went down to the street. I had these things in mind—look for her car, hold a parking place, be there waving when she turned into the block.

At a quarter to five, I came back up. I changed my shirt. I wiped off my shoes. I looked into the mirror to see if I looked like someone's father.

She presented herself shortly after six o'clock.

"Traffic?" I said. "No," she said, and that was the end of that.

Just as supper was being concluded, she complained of insufferable pain, and doubled over on the dining-room floor.

"My belly," she said. "What?" I said. She said, "My belly. It's agony. Get me a doctor."

There is a large and famous hospital mere blocks from my apartment. Celebrities go there, statesmen, people who must know what they are doing.

With the help of a doorman and an elevator man, I got my daughter to the hospital. Within minutes, two physicians and a corps of nurses took the matter in hand.

I stood by watching. It was hours before they had her undoubled and were willing to announce their findings.

A bellyache, a rogue cramp, a certain nonspecific seizure of the abdomen—vagrant, indecipherable, a mystery not worth further inquiry.

We left the hospital unassisted, using a succession of tunnels in order to shorten the distance home. The exposed distance, that is—since it would be four in the morning on the city streets, and though the blocks would be few, each one of them could be catastrophic. So we made our way along the system of underground passageways that link the units of the hospital until we were forced to surface and exit. We came out onto a street with not a person on it—until we saw him, the young man who was going from car to car. He carried something under his arm. It looked to me to be a furled umbrella—black fabric, silver fittings.

It could not have been what it looked to be—but instead a tool of entry disguised as an umbrella!

He turned to us as we stepped along, and then he turned back to his work—going from car to car, trying the doors, and sometimes using the thing to dig at the windows.

"Don't look," I said. My daughter said, "What?" I said, "There's someone across the street. He's trying to jimmy open cars. Just keep on walking as if you don't see him."

My daughter said, "Where? I don't see him."

I put my daughter to bed and the hospital charges on my desk and then I let my head down onto the pillow and listened.

There was nothing to hear.

Before I surrendered myself to sleep, there was only this in my mind—the boy in the treatment room across the corridor from my daughter's, how I had wanted to cry out each time he had cried out as a stitch was sutured into his hand.

"Take it out! Take it out!"

This is what the boy was shrieking as the doctor worked to close the wound.

I thought about the feeling in me when I had heard that awful wailing. The boy wanted the needle out. I suppose it hurt worse than the thing that had inspired them to sew him up.

But then I considered the statement for emergency services—translating the amount first into theater tickets, then into hand-ironed shirts.

Kate McCorkle

THE LAST
PARAKEET

I think the last Pyrruhura parakeet is about to make a statement. The camera has moved in on him so that he takes up the whole TV screen, and his black eyes, first one, then the other, have me fixed at my breakfast table. He is pink and green but he has blue shadows under his eyes just like all the guests on the "Today" show because it's so early there in the New York studio. He is gripping the finger of a Brazilian biologist with his wiry yellow feet. While I pour the milk on my Rice Krispies, they flash a little sign under him, BRAZILIAN PARAKEET, LAST OF SPECIES. They say he turned himself in.

There is a little surreptitious knock at my door, a knock trying not to be a knock once it has called attention to itself. That will be my neighbor, Hattie, from across the hall. Hattie is a single lady. I carry my bowl of Krispies with me, walking backwards to the door, keeping an eye on the TV. The little knock comes again and I open the door with a jerk. Hattie's there in a fuzzy pink bathrobe with a green towel around her head. I have to look at her because this is an uncommon sight. Generally, I see Hattie at dusk, in a sort of mating ritual, taking some man in off the doorstep. They always look drabber than she does and a bit deaf to the call. Hattie asks without blinking for the Worcestershire sauce. I don't inquire what for.

When I get back to my TV of course they have gone on to something else, namely ways in which divorced women can turn hobbies into fortunes. One of them is there on the screen looking pleased with herself and the subtitle under her says DIVORCÉE MILLIONAIRE. Bryant Gumble asks her if it isn't just a little vulgar to leave a marriage and then make all that money.

I sit down at my table and pull my feet up under me. I'm not even putting this milk away until I hear what that parakeet has to say. I play with my watch trying to figure what time it is in Brazil. He must have made his decision sometime deep in the night. Then he fluttered out of the dark and threw himself against the biologist's windows, I imagine, like a giant pink moth. My guess is that the loneliness got to him.

I wonder how he figured out that he *was* alone. Did he fly all around the rain forest looking into other bird faces for one like his own? Or did it just dawn on him one day, amidst all the screeching and crying?

Willard Scott comes on with the weather. This is one of his secure, toupee-less days. He's got a picture of Elvira Hoopsmart, who is one hundred years old today in Ascot, Pennsylvania. He makes the camera come in real close on Elvira so we can see her little black eyes. She's beautiful, Willard notes, but he doesn't mention who turned her in for being one hundred. This species is safe, I think, unless Willard has a whole drawer full of old pictures and just makes the names up every day.

There's a sharp little knock on my door which I surmise to be made with the aid of a Worcestershire sauce bottle. Hattie is all dressed up for work now with high heels and a white blouse up to her chin, and blue, blue shadows under her eyes. They never ask the questions you want answers to on these shows.

There he is. It's the 8:30 news roundup, just the essence, you know, of everything. "Here are some of the stories we're working on for you." The president is there for a second and a couple of hangdog astronauts and somebody in the hospital being given new hope and some handcuffed kid looking at the ground. There's a long shot this time of the Brazilian biologist lounging in his chair and holding his finger out at Bryant. The parakeet looks so small. Time does not permit us to hear his version.

Paul Lisicky

SNAPSHOT,
HARVEY CEDARS:
1948

My mother touches her forehead, throwing her green eyes into shade. Her mouth is pink, her hair blond like wheat. She is tanned. She is the best-looking woman on the beach, only she will never recognize it. She wraps her long body in an aqua sarong and winces, believes her hips are a bell. Even now she is counting, waiting for the camera to flicker shut.

My father's arm weights down her shoulder. He is muscular, his stomach flat as a pan. He looks full ahead, pretending he is with my mother, but already he is in Florida, developing new

cities, pumping dead mangrove full of sand. He sees himself building, building. He will be healthy. He will have good fortune. And
years in the future, after his Army buddies will have grown soft
and womanish, all his hard work will pay off: people will remember
his name.

Their shoulders touch. Their pose says: this is how young
couples are supposed to look—see, aren't we the lucky ones? But
my mother's head is tilted. What is she looking at? Is she gazing
at the tennis player by the outdoor shower, the one with the
gentle hands, the one who will teach her to unlearn things? Or
can she already hear the gun which my father will press into his
forehead, twenty years away?

Joyce Carol Oates

AUGUST
EVENING

He drives a new-model metallic-blue Cougar with all the accessories including air conditioning and a tape deck and beige kidskin interior plus some special things of his own for instance a compass affixed to his dashboard, a special blind-spot mirror, extra strips of chrome around the windows and license plates, a glitter-flecked steering wheel "spin," and, in cold weather, a steering wheel covering made of snakeskin. In warm weather he likes to cruise the city as he'd done twenty years ago or maybe more except now he's alone and not with his friends as he'd been back then. As if nothing has changed and the surprise is that not much really has changed in certain parts of the city and off the larger streets and he's drawn back always a little expectant and curious to the old places for instance St. Mary's Church where they'd all gone and the grammar school next door, the half-dozen houses his parents had rented while he and his brothers were growing up though he couldn't name their chronological sequence any longer and one or two of them have been remodeled, glitzy fake-brick siding and big picture windows so it's difficult to recognize the houses except by way of the neighboring houses which are beginning to be unrecognizable too. There's a variety store close by the school hardly changed at all where he parks to get a pack of Luckies and just as he's leaving he runs into this woman Jacky he'd known in high school back before she was married and he was married and she's in tight shorts that show the swell of her buttocks and her small round stomach and a tank-top blouse like a young girl would wear looking good with her fleshy smiling mouth and her eyes shadowed in silvery blue and her legs still long and trim though a little bunchy at the knees. At first it almost seems Jacky doesn't recognize him then of course she does and they get to talking and laughing and it's clear she likes him looking at her like that asking him questions about his job and where he's living now since the divorce and what's his ex-wife doing, and then they get to talking about old friends and high school classmates, guys he hung around with, some of them they haven't seen or heard of in years so you'd wonder are they still alive but better not ask. And gradually they run out of things to say but neither wants to break away just yet they're smiling so hard at each other and standing a little closer than you'd ordinarily stand, Jacky's the kind of woman likes to touch a man's arm when she talks, and he's thinking a thought he'd had before and probably she has too that the marriages by now are more or less interchangeable like objects blurring in a rearview mirror as you speed away but also it's the warm lazy air smelling of soft tar from the streets and sirens in the distance or is it a freight train like those childhood sounds you'd hear at night . . . melancholy and sweet-sounding with the power to make your eyes fill with tears. And they see themselves off somewhere hurriedly undressing . . . and the frantic hungry coupling . . . and the orgasm protracted for each as in slow motion . . . and the sweaty stunned aftermath, the valedictory kisses, caresses, stammered words . . . All that they aren't going to do but they're locked together seeing it and Jacky's eyes look dilated and he's feeling the impact of it as if somebody were pushing hard on his chest with an opened hand so that he almost can't breathe.

Honey was that *sweet* are the words he isn't going to say and Jacky can't think of what to say either so they back off from each other and she says "Take care" and he says "Okay—you too" and he gets in his car and drives off sad-feeling and excited and eager to be gone all at once—knowing not to bother looking for her in the rearview mirror, he's accelerating so fast.

Mary Dilworth

THE FACTORY

I have always hated the factory. It has a gaunt steel frame like a skeleton. I've often imagined it without its red bricks, just an etching of black against a red sky.

Of course, I've never said anything about this to anyone. Especially to Eric. You see, he loves the factory. He would like to put up his sign in those flashing neon lights that the city firms can afford. He saw a rainbow once over a petrol station there. I think he would have sold almost anything to have one of those on his roof.

Every day he is up early. He sings in the shower and eats his breakfast quietly. He always reads the business section of the newspaper, then quarters it neatly.

His days are like that. In four parts.

The first is the morning, which I've mentioned. Then there's the day at the factory. That's in two: the morning and the afternoon.

He uses the telephone to tell me when it's time for lunch. Just two rings. That's his code. Then five minutes later he's at the door, letting himself in.

He reads at lunch, usually one of the classics. He didn't have much education.

In fact, that's why I met him. We worked at the same factory, ten miles out of town. It manufactured shoes and boots. I was the boss's secretary, and Eric worked the floor.

I'll always remember that first day. He was nervous, tried not to show it, but his hands shook. His hair was brown, his eyes were brown, and the factory overalls were brown. He almost faded into the background of brown leather shoes. Which was quite funny at the time.

But I was describing his day. And he's not brown any more. Streaks of gray and a balding patch which he rakes over, spreading the hairs thinly across it. And he wears a suit. Usually gray, with a red handkerchief in the pocket. I suppose his eyes are still the same color, but I can't tell you. If you asked me, I just couldn't tell you. I did notice they were red tonight, which was unusual, but then the whole day was different. As though the four quarters came together and just rolled away.

I could draw the second half of his day with my eyes closed.

In the afternoon, he has a cup of tea in his office, then he works until six o'clock.

Two rings on the telephone mean he's coming home for dinner. He has a good appetite and enjoys his food.

In the evening he likes quiet. He always says that after such a busy day at the factory, he needs to sit and think. Which he does, with his eyes closed, his elbow on the chair, and his thumb and one finger pressed against his forehead. Or sometimes he just sits and stares into space.

Eric always goes to bed early. He feels fresh then for the next day.

But now the next day won't come. It won't be Eric's day, and his eyes are red. I've never seen him cry before.

I said this day was different. It's night now, and soon the dawn will come. In the night, the sky was red. A brilliant red. That was beautiful. Black against red. Like a devil with horns or the final crashing chords of a great concerto.

I loved it. Black skeleton of steel in a fiery night. Of course the fire brigade came. I didn't call them. It was beautiful just watching the sky burning. I don't think I will ever forget it. Eric was asleep.

They came to tell us as soon as they arrived. Eric knew straight away it was all over.

I love the night. Sometimes I stay up for hours, savoring it. The stars and that great arc of sky. The immense pattern, the changing moods of wind.

Tonight it was special. It was different. And I feel very tired. But happy. An exhilarated feeling, a prickling right down my spine.

Nobody knows how the fire started. Accidental, they say. It happens all the time.

THE SEWERS OF SALT LAKE

Let's taste each other's bodies now without pleasure," Martha says.

The living room is full of our dogs. It's evening and the young men from the gas company are lined up in the street singing a Jerry Lee Lewis medley. They've got the grand piano strapped on the back of a flatbed truck parked under the maple trees. They sing like fallen angels. *Breathless. Great Balls of Fire. Hang Up My Rock 'n' Roll Shoes.*

"Touch me here," Martha says. *High School Confidential. There's a*

Whole Lot of Shakin' Goin' On. They're all castrati, with those thin pure high voices that specify otherness and absence.

"Baby, baby, baby," Martha says.

I accuse her of bad faith. "You said without pleasure."

"It came over me like a big wind," Martha apologizes.

She looks skeletal without her clothes on. Ribs like an anatomy lesson. I love her, but what can I do? This morning I made *fajitas* and she picked out all the bits of chicken, sailed her tortillas like Frisbees to the grateful dogs. Toyed with a piece of green pepper, satisfied herself with slivers of onion.

Tomorrow afternoon it's the Utah Power and Light people doing Janis Joplin. Big women in meter-reader uniforms singing the blues.

On the far side of the room, under the moiling dogs the twins play. One says "Mama." The other answers "Mama. Mama."

The dogs have dug a complicated system of tunnels in the backyard. They hide during the day in the cool underground dark, and pop up at unpredictable intervals like small hairy Viet Cong. This morning the twins disappeared in the labyrinth and Martha put on her camouflage fatigues and went down after them. It's been three hours now, and I'm waiting for her to return. There's a light rain falling all over Utah; the state is damp and almost uninhabitable. Martha took the rechargeable flashlight and a box of Ritz crackers in case she had to stay past lunchtime. Mishka and Mishka, the twins, have always loved to explore dark places; I'm not worried. The dogs will look after them until Martha arrives.

Later I look out the window and see Martha coming out of the entrance under the gooseberry bushes. She's crawling on all fours, carrying Mishka in her teeth by the back of his overalls.

"Where's Mishka?" I say.

"The dogs are bringing him up. They've carved out little rooms down there, with tiny beds and candlesticks made out of empty C-ration cans. It's comfortable and warm, not at all what I expected."

At the entrance to the sewers, in the basement of the county courthouse, a sign forbids the public to pick up anything they might find and take it home. The corporation guides wear their dress uniforms; instead of the billed caps they have on miners' helmets with powerful carbide lamps. Martha carries Mishka in a sling, tucked against her belly; I carry Mishka in a backpack.

"Mama," Mishka says.

"Mama, Mama," the other Mishka answers.

The compulsory tour is given once a year to citizens chosen by lot from the voter registration rolls. We are happy to be here, though we wish they had allowed us to leave the babies at home. Martha reads to me from her leaflet:

"Various nocturnal animals may be encountered in the tunnels and must on no account be fed or petted or disturbed in any manner. Respect the ecology of the sewers."

The guides walk close to us, nightsticks drawn in case we become recalcitrant. The one nearest to Martha frowns when she stumbles, and pushes her back in line, but not unkindly.

We are in the Baptist Catacombs, under Sears and Roebuck. Luminous skulls are set in niches all along the walls. Loose pieces of Baptists have fallen from their resting places and are scattered underfoot. The small finger bones crack like twigs when we step on them.

We arrive under the Temple in time to experience, from beneath, the ritual rinsing of the baptismal fonts. The rush of holy water through the golden pipes startles the twins; Martha gives them suck, one on each breast.

A crocodile drifts slowly down the stream a few feet away, eyes and nostrils barely above the dark waters. A woman in a calico dress throws him a slice of Wonder Bread and the guards strike her down with their sticks. Softly at first, but with increasing fervor, we sing old Eric Clapton songs. *After Midnight. Layla. Bell-Bottom Blues.*

Steven Molen

JANE

Rachel is the one whose hair is golden like Mother's. They wear it in the same way, freely, without braids or bobby pins. Her hands are Mother's, too, white and smooth. They are hands to be held, not to hold, and her eyes are wet and bright, like pools of water. That blue. People say that Rachel is beautiful. She says yes by how she spreads a napkin on her lap and lifts a fork neatly to her lips. After brushing her teeth and combing that hair, she stands at the mirror and studies herself, practices a smile. My watching doesn't stop her. She likes an audience.

Now that she's gone, I can stand here, too. I have the bottom floor to myself: the two bedrooms (hers and mine) and the bathroom with its mirror. In another week, I will have the whole house. Mother and Father are going to visit her. It is not a vacation, says Mother, only a house in the country where girls like Rachel stay, a school that teaches them to forget and be girls again.

Mother says that forgetting is hard. The bruises are gone, but Rachel still bleeds in her thoughts. This can only be healed by the quiet hours of the country house. At night, when the darkness returns her to that other night, the nurses can help. Without them, the remembering would smother her. Mother and Father tried to lift it off, but it was too heavy. It came every night those two weeks she was home. I could hear her whimper through the wall. The sound of a baby without milk. The bed creaked as she rocked herself in a cradle made of her own arms. After the screaming began, Mother and Father would run downstairs to shake her awake and hold her. They stopped the screaming but never the low whimper. It came from deep inside, and must have been a roaring in her head.

Rachel could be a mother by Christmas. Like a nightmare, it is not something that will stop on its own. It can only grow. Rachel is young, just eighteen. Mother was twenty-eight when Rachel was born, almost thirty with me. Everyone knows there will have to be an abortion, but Mother still wonders what the baby would be like. After all, the baby is not just Rachel. It is half the man. Would the new, little fingers feel rough? We are told that in the country house Rachel talks about things from the past: our old songbird and the dollhouse we had. Her appetite is good, but this is the baby eating.

In the dollhouse, I remember, Rachel and Jane were two dolls exactly the same, and our babies were smaller dolls the size of erasers. They, too, were all the same. Since Mother never bought us doll men, our husbands were always at work. We would wait for them on the tiny porch just as Mother used to, standing at the window, looking out for Father.

Now they are getting ready to leave. Although Mother is busy, she writes a list of things for me to remember: water the plants, feed Domino, and bring in the paper. The last part is important. Nobody should know that I am alone. I need to lock the doors at night and make sure all the windows are closed. Mother holds my hand and says this is difficult for all of us. Her hand is like a small bird caught in mine. We talk about what I am doing in school and the watercolors I paint. While I tell her about the self-portrait I want to do, we make dinner together. Father will come home soon, and then we will eat. They are leaving tomorrow.

Most girls would like this. Rachel would. She'd invite her friends over and listen to their music on Father's stereo. I can see them smoking pot and joking about boys. That's what Rachel would do, or have a boy over by herself. But Rachel is gone. I will tear up Mother's list, let the begonias starve in their pots, Domino cry at the neighbor's house for milk, and the papers pile up on the drive. I will smile naked in the mirror, at every lighted window, my hair loose and dark on my shoulders, and one night I will hear a door open somewhere in the empty house and then, soft like the branches on my window before a storm, footsteps on the stairs: his at first, then Mother and Father's rushing after.

Marlene Buono

OFFERINGS

Emily often felt invisible. Only yesterday she had been at the dentist's office waiting patiently for her three o'clock appointment. At three-fifteen Mr. Mackley was called. At four, Debby Chapman. At four-fifteen she asked the nurse why her name hadn't been called. The nurse's face turned red and she was lavish with her apologies. Emily caught one of them as they flew around the room and added it to her collection.

People were always saying they were sorry to her. Last week while having a permanent, she watched in the mirror as the hairdresser removed the curlers, and frizzled tufts of hair fell to the ground. The hairdresser cried. Emily comforted her and accepted a complimentary wig to wear until her hair grew out. The hairdresser insisted she take several apologies and Emily obliged her, but on the way out she left two of them on the magazine rack.

The butcher was sorry he didn't have round, would lamb steaks do? The cleaner was sorry he couldn't remove the marinara sauce from her silk blouse, she should have brought it in sooner. The ad agency liked her portfolio, but regretted that they weren't hiring for another few months. The doctor was sorry, her husband's tumor was inoperable.

Some days she could fit all the apologies into her purse, but most days she had to stuff the overflow into her pockets and under her wig. Sometimes she cut them into circles and dropped them into the coin rolls she picked up at the bank.

One day, about two years after her husband died, she received a postcard that read:

WE'RE SORRY YOU DIDN'T WIN FIRST OR SECOND PRIZE
IN THE SWEEPSTAKES YOU ENTERED. AS A THANKS FOR
ENTERING, HOWEVER, YOUR LOCAL BOOKSTORE HAS
A SPECIAL GIFT TO YOU FROM US. JUST SHOW THEM
THIS CARD.

The next time Emily went downtown she stopped into the bookstore to pick up her gift. The clerk said he was sorry, the store had run out of the original prizes, but she could have an overstocked paperback on the art of origami. Emily was going to let the clerk keep his apology since she felt that getting the book was enough, but he just left it on the counter so she picked it up and used it as a bookmark.

On the bus ride home she took out the book and her day's collection of sorries. She practiced on the small apologies first, folding them into ducks and cranes and owls. Some of them were cumbersome and difficult to tame. Others were easy and almost creased themselves. Following the book closely, Emily refused to use scissors and as a result a few of the apologies could not be trained. These she sewed to the hem of her skirt.

She was so busy that she missed her stop. The bus driver told her he was sorry, but she'd have to get off and take another bus since he was going back to the yard.

That night she couldn't sleep. She rummaged through her closet and put on the dining room table all of the apologies she had collected. By candlelight and without the book to guide her, Emily folded the regrets into hundreds of winged creatures. The more she folded, the more skilled she became. She even removed the sloppy apologies that were sewn to her skirts and fashioned them into pterodactyls.

The next day was April 29th, the day she always visited her husband's grave. Emily hired a taxi to take her to the cemetery. While passing through the gates the driver said, "Sorry, I can't wait for you, but I've got to pick up a fare at the airport. Give us a call when you're ready."

She waved him on after quickly folding what he had given her into a butterfly.

Emily trimmed the grass around her husband's gravestone and washed the bird droppings from the marble. She tried to remember the sound of his laughter and the way he used to scan her body with both hands. She tried to imagine a conversation they might have after making love.

Even though the dampness of the earth made her think of bones and dust and gravity, she tried to picture her husband in heaven, as one of the clouds that roamed the sky.

She opened the hatbox she had brought along and lifted out an apology that she had meant to give her husband before he died. It was an awkward shape and she rarely looked at it because it filled her with shame. She deftly folded the edges until the perimeter of the regret was smooth. Emily studied the apology before each fold, carefully coaxing it to forget its graceless form and accept her design.

She took an hour to give it the wingspan it needed. When she placed the finished apology on the gravestone she watched it unfold its wings and fly.

Margaret Atwood

BREAD

Imagine a piece of bread. You don't have to imagine it, it's right here in the kitchen, on the breadboard, in its plastic bag, lying beside the bread knife. The bread knife is an old one you picked up at an auction; it has the word BREAD carved into the wooden handle. You open the bag, pull back the wrapper, cut yourself a slice. You put butter on it, then peanut butter, then honey, and you fold it over. Some of the honey runs out onto your fingers and you lick it off. It takes you about a minute to eat the bread. This bread happens to be brown, but there is also white bread, in the refrigerator, and a heel of rye you got last week, round as a full stomach then, now going moldy. Occasionally you make bread. You think of it as something relaxing to do with your hands.

Imagine a famine. Now imagine a piece of bread. Both of these things are real but you happen to be in the same room with only one of them. Put yourself into a different room, that's what the mind is for. You are now lying on a thin mattress in a hot room. The walls are made of dried earth, and your sister, who is younger than you, is in the room with you. She is starving, her belly is bloated, flies land on her eyes; you brush them off with your hand. You have a cloth too, filthy but damp, and you press it to her lips and forehead. The piece of bread is the bread you've been saving, for days it seems. You are as hungry as she is, but not yet as weak. How long does this take? When will someone come with more bread? You think of going out to see if you might find something that could be eaten, but outside the streets are infested with scavengers and the stink of corpses is everywhere.

Should you share the bread or give the whole piece to your sister? Should you eat the piece of bread yourself? After all, you have a better chance of living, you're stronger. How long does it take to decide?

Imagine a prison. There is something you know that you have not yet told. Those in control of the prison know that you know. So do those not in control. If you tell, thirty or forty or a hundred of your friends, your comrades, will be caught and will die. If you refuse to tell, tonight will be like last night. They always choose the night. You don't think about the night however, but about the piece of bread they offered you. How long does it take? The piece of bread was brown and fresh and reminded you of sunlight falling across a wooden floor. It reminded you of a bowl, a yellow bowl that was once in your home. It held apples and pears; it stood on a table you can also remember. It's not the hunger or the pain that is killing you but the absence of the yellow bowl. If you could only hold the bowl in your hands, right here, you could withstand anything, you tell yourself. The bread they offered you is subversive, it's treacherous, it does not mean life.

There were once two sisters. One was rich and had no children, the other had five children and was a widow, so poor that she no longer had any food left. She went to her sister and asked her for a mouthful of bread. "My children are dying," she said. The rich sister said, "I do not have enough for myself," and drove her away from the door. Then the husband of the rich sister came home and wanted to cut himself a piece of bread; but when he made the first cut, out flowed red blood.

Everyone knew what that meant.

This is a traditional German fairy tale.

The loaf of bread I have conjured for you floats about a foot above your kitchen table. The table is normal, there are no trap doors in it. A blue tea towel floats beneath the bread, and there are no strings attaching the cloth to the bread or the bread to the ceiling or the table to the cloth, you've proved it by passing your hand above and below. You didn't touch the bread though. What stopped you? You don't want to know whether the bread is real or whether it's just a hallucination I've somehow duped you into seeing. There's no doubt that you can see the bread, you can even smell it, it smells like yeast, and it looks solid enough, solid as your own arm. But can you trust it? Can you eat it? You don't want to know, imagine that.

Ronald Wallace

YOGURT

They were fighting more than usual lately, or perhaps fighting had just become usual, he thought, as they walked home from Yogurt Express along the dark side street. There was no moon, and in the darkness the houses loomed huge and unfamiliar.

He was thinking about earlier in the week, at the grocery, when they'd fought over the sugar cereal. He'd tossed it into the cart, and she'd taken it out, reprimanding him.

"I don't want you buying this crap," she'd said.

"Jesus," he'd replied, wheeling off cockeyed down the aisle. "What are you anyway, my mother?"

These petty clashes rankled him more and more, and he held on to them for days, replaying every nuance and detail, running his mind over them like a tongue on a sore tooth.

Now, as they walked along the quiet street, not touching, he thought what it would be like to live alone, all that freedom. The idea of a separation—he with his own space, his own time, his own decisions—increasingly gave him pleasure. There were, of course, the complications of the kids, the house, the two cars, the bank account, the country property, but was that any reason to stay together?

A rapid slap of feet on pavement just behind them brought him up short, and, as he turned, startled, a cup of cold yogurt slashed into his face, blinding him.

"Hey!" he shouted.

A dark shape scurried past, turning the corner. "I *hate* couples!" it snarled and disappeared.

He felt weak, his breath uneven. "What was *that?*" he said, wiping yogurt from his eyes and chin.

She was silent a moment, and then, "I've seen him before," she said. "In the daytime. He wears a skullcap, and sort of slinks around. I thought he was harmless."

"Jesus, it's such a . . . a . . ."

"Violation?" She gave him the word he was looking for.

"Yes, a violation. I wonder if we should report him. Warn the children. Lock our doors."

They had reached the corner, but no one was there. In the light of the street lamp, she looked serene, and, he thought, well, *valuable.* He put his arm around her and drew her close. Slowly, she put her arm around him.

Pavao Pavlicić

A CHRONICLER'S SIN

Once upon a time, during the reign of terror, mass arrests became the order of the day. Most often they took place at night: a group of hooded men would knock at the front door and order the sleepy host to get dressed, and then take him to one of the many small prisons mushrooming all over the town. Sometimes the policemen would arrest whole families, including the children and grandmothers who slept on the hearths.

The population of the town was shrinking, and all night long saber-rattling patrols could be heard leading the people away through the streets, from a great many houses. Many people began to spend their nights fully clothed, dozing with bundles under their heads as if traveling, expecting to be arrested. People were amazed that there was so much room in prisons, but then one house after another was turned into a prison, and one person would languish in another's house as if in jail: the rich in poor people's quarters and the other way around, soldiers in schools, priests in barracks, doctors and patients in brothels, debauchees in convents.

There was an increasing shortage of labor, and prisoners did most of the jobs. Since they were dressed like other people and their numbers were kept secret, it was difficult to know who was a prisoner and who was free. The prisoners were even employed to make arrests: they carried sabers although they were prisoners.

The number of arrests was rising—among the next victims were members of the notorious City Authorities. Priests, merchants, chiefs of staff, sentries, clerks, and others were taken away. In the end they were all made prisoners, even the members of the Administration themselves. Everybody spied on each other; everybody was a prisoner and nobody knew who was actually in charge, issuing these orders and arrest warrants. Everybody had the feeling that he was taking part in the running of the town, in the arrests and in the serving of time in prison. And as all of them were dressed alike and enjoyed the same rights—all of them being under arrest—they went on doing their jobs as if nothing had happened. They lived their ordinary lives and, had someone asked them, they would probably have said they were happy.

Several years later they would deny that any arrests had been made at all and claim that it was all a fabrication of an inadequately censored, and undoubtedly malicious, chronicler.

Translated by Miroslav Beker

S. *Friedman*

HERE

Elvis lives three houses away. We don't have houses
exactly, they're metal sheds, corrugated, very shiny, with nothing
inside except us, when we're there. We wave Hi in the mornings
and evenings like any workaday neighbors, but there are no lawns
to discuss, or sports, or even weather, so waving's about it for
social life here. The two sheds between us are officially vacant,
the sliding doors wide open on bare cement, so if we did talk it
might be about who lived there last, or who's about to live there,
but the fact is that even here and now I'm in too much silly awe

to attempt small talk with a dead legend. I'd naively expected to meet my parents here, or pretty Nancy who developed a brain tumor in my second grade, but we seem to be on our own with a vengeance, the only exceptions being as I say these neighbors we see before and after work. What we are is complete strangers with identical schedules.

I don't know where anyone else goes or comes back from. Next door on the other side I have a very short woman, possibly a dwarf, who wears boxy little dresses of a 1940s cut and carries a blue aluminum lunch pail. Unlike Elvis she always throws me a genuine smile that warms me with its gallantry and lack of self-pity. Beyond her lives a burly Sikh with a turban who clears his sinuses loudly as we set off on our separate ways. No one goes in the same direction as anyone else. We all walk straight ahead but the horizon seems to widen so that our paths diverge and we soon disappear from each other. I have a fairly pleasant job but it takes me a long time to get there; I never know how far I have to go because the route is always some new combination of all the walks of my life—through the woods behind my first remembered house, up the cast iron stairs to my father's law office, across my high school playground, down the driveway of my second wife's condo after she married again. All these places are quite deserted except for me. And eventually, in one of these settings, I see my bench, with the day's task laid out for me, self-explanatory, some variation of a simple mindless chore I performed in a shop course, like soldering, or a tray of letters to case out from my days in the post office. It's good to work; I have no complaints on that score. But I must say that the fact of Elvis so near and yet so far distracts and preoccupies me at my labors.

I have no idea if I am unique. It may be that everyone here has Elvis living three doors away and has to confront that situation

in his or her own fashion. It may be only those like me who
played his records to annoy their fathers and had those records
confiscated or broken in two, or those like me again who used
his mystique on girls of thirteen or fourteen with bad intentions,
who now have to face him first and last thing every day, and
decide what to say to him. Or it may be that I alone, out of how
many billions, by sheer chance am the nearest neighbor of this
illustrious figure. The question in any case remains how do I make
the most of it?

And every day, bending my sheet of tin or aligning my crisp
envelopes, I am rehearsing my first approach. I will not pry or
invade his privacy. I will brighten his day, as the dwarf lady does
mine. Sometimes I ponder an apropos line from one of his hits.
"Takin' a walk down Lonely Street!" I might call out. I try this
aloud at my bench; it gives me shudders. Should I tell him he's
looking good? He must know he isn't. Most mornings he has
trouble getting his door open and has to pause for breath before
he closes it behind him. When he takes off his shades to check
the sky his eyes are puffed almost shut. But his self-assurance is
something to behold. If he were a rotted corpse, if he were a
skeleton, he'd still be Elvis. Wherever he goes is the right place
for him. I'd like to tell him that in simple casual words that don't
crown him with the thorns of his fame all over again. But the fact
is I probably won't.

Every day both ways the commute seems to get longer, for all
of us. We're starting earlier and getting home later with, for me
at least, less and less actual work time. This may be a reward or
a punishment. But it doesn't leave much margin for conversation.
It's getting so we're mere shadows to each other at the crack of
dawn and the tag end of dusk. This evening out of desperation I
waved with two hands as if I had a message for him and he paused,

just a big bulky shape in a fringed jacket with his hand on his door, and waited to hear me. "Home," I said. "Home at last." I could barely make him out but I believe he aimed his forefinger at me and lowered his thumb, like a cowboy. That was sweet. That was him all over. He knows me.

Diane Williams

HERE'S
ANOTHER
ENDING

This time my story has a foregone conclusion.

It is true also.

After I tell the story, I say, "You could start a religion based on a story like that—couldn't you?"

The story begins with my idea of a huge dog—a Doberman —which is to me an emblem—cruel, not lovable.

The dog is a household pet in a neighborhood such as mine, with houses with backyards which abut.

The huge dog is out and about when it should not be. It should never be.

When the dog returns to its owners, it is carrying in its mouth a dirty dead rabbit.

The dog's owners exclaim—one of them does—"The neighbor's rabbit! He's killed it!" The dog's owners conclude, "We must save our dog's reputation at all costs." They think, Our dog is in jeopardy.

The dog's owners shampoo the dead rabbit and dry it with a hair dryer. At night, they sneak the rabbit back into their neighbor's yard, into its cage.

The morning of the following day, the dog's owners hear a shriek from the rabbit owners' yard. They think, Oh! The dead rabbit has been discovered! They rush to see what's what.

One of the rabbit's owners—the father in the family—is holding the limp, white rabbit up in the air. He says to the dog's owners, "We buried her two days ago!"

The dog's owners explain nothing. They won't, but not because they are ashamed of themselves.

There is another, more obvious reason.

108 JOHN STREET

The house was yellow. The days were long. The kitchen was crowded sometimes. Bill knew a way to tie up the paper bags of trash with string but Mark could never master it. This was an amusing issue on Wednesday nights. The refrigerator hummed softly. Mark went upstairs and found Jessica in their gray-carpeted room listening to Carole King. Her hair was wet and very dark. She said, "Did you eat the pie, Monkey?" Bill took a shower while Judy waited for him in the larger bedroom. Judy thought Bill took an unnaturally long time in the shower. Through the bathroom door she would shout *"William."* Jessica told Mark that Judy was jealous of hot running water. Mark typed a very flimsy poem in green ink. The poem implied that certain persons, like him, were able to see angels in the air, while others couldn't. He moved some books from one pile to another. He doubted that he would ever read *The Death of Artemio Cruz* and wondered if he should feel depressed about this. When Lena Chen came over and cooked food in the wok, Mark always chopped the onions. "Monkey cries whenever Chen the Wren visits us," said Jessica. She drew a cartoon of pigs wearing overalls eating ice cream sodas. In the basement room, Lawrence the gay lawyer spoke on the phone about Mozart as if no one else had ever heard of Mozart. In the kitchen Lawrence liked to use the phrase "quality cookware." The night he announced that he was gay, everybody had to act serious. They were learning to live together. Bill pointed out to Mark that he often neglected to wash the bottoms of dishes and pans. Bill read a murder mystery soberly, missing no clues. The living room was surprisingly pleasant with a sand-colored sofa and Lawrence's quality lamps. All of this, all of this, Jessica with her brown eyes so awake, all of this was significant, all of it vibrated just below consciousness with a strong significance. Or was it only life? Only life? Mark ate celery with cheese and then joined Jessica upstairs. She was joking on the phone, something about Simone de Beauvoir telling Jean-Paul to straighten up and fly right. Mark meant to read something about Vietnam but he was sleepy. Jessica mocked him for singing "Please Please Me" off-key but when she hugged him life was good. In the morning a pigeon patrolled the windowsill very near their sleeping heads. All significant. And God put it all in a cloth bag and swung it around and tossed it lightly into the river.

DEPORTATION
AT BREAKFAST

The signs on the windows lured me inside. For a dollar I could get two eggs, toast, and potatoes. The place looked better than most—family-run and clean. The signs were hand-lettered and neat. The paper had yellowed some, but the black letters remained bold. A green-and-white awning was perched over the door, where the name "Clara's" was stenciled.

Inside, the place had an appealing and old-fashioned look. The air smelled fresh and homey, not greasy. The menu was printed on a chalkboard. It was short and to the point. It listed the kinds of toast you could choose from. One entry was erased from the middle of the list. By deduction, I figured it was rye. I didn't want rye toast anyway.

Because I was alone, I sat at the counter, leaving the empty tables free for other customers that might come in. At the time, business was quiet. Only two tables were occupied, and I was alone at the counter. But it was still early—not yet seven-thirty.

Behind the counter was a short man with dark black hair, a mustache, and a youthful beard, one that never grew much past stubble. He was dressed immaculately, all in chef's white—pants, shirt, and apron, but no hat. He had a thick accent. The name "Javier" was stitched on his shirt.

I ordered coffee, and asked for a minute to choose between the breakfast special for a dollar and the cheese omelette for $1.59. I selected the omelette.

The coffee was hot, strong, and fresh. I spread my newspaper on the counter and sipped at the mug as Javier went to the grill to cook my meal.

The eggs were spread out on the griddle, the bread plunged inside the toaster, when the authorities came in. They grabbed Javier quickly and without a word, forcing his hands behind his back. He, too, said nothing. He did not resist, and they shoved him out the door and into their waiting car.

On the grill, my eggs bubbled. I looked around for another employee—maybe out back somewhere, or in the washroom. I leaned over the counter and called for someone. No one answered. I looked behind me toward the tables. Two elderly men sat at one, two elderly women at the other. The two women were talking. The men were reading the paper. They seemed not to have noticed Javier's exit.

I could smell my eggs starting to burn. I wasn't quite sure what to do about it. I thought about Javier and stared at my eggs. After some hesitation, I got up from my red swivel stool and went behind the counter. I grabbed a spare apron, then picked up the spatula and turned my eggs. My toast had popped up, but it was not browned, so I put it down again. While I was cooking, the two elderly women came to the counter and asked to pay. I asked what they had had. They seemed surprised that I didn't remember. I checked the prices on the chalkboard and rang up their order. They paid slowly, fishing through large purses, and went out, leaving me a dollar tip. I took my eggs off the grill and slid them onto a clean plate. My toast had come up. I buttered it and put it on my plate beside my eggs. I put the plate at my spot at the counter, right next to my newspaper.

As I began to come back from behind the counter to my stool, six new customers came through the door. "Can we pull some tables together?" they asked. "We're all one party." I told them yes. Then they ordered six coffees, two decaffeinated.

I thought of telling them I didn't work there. But perhaps they were hungry. I poured their coffee. Their order was simple: six breakfast specials, all with scrambled eggs and wheat toast. I got busy at the grill.

Then the elderly men came to pay. More new customers began arriving. By eight-thirty, I had my hands full. With this kind of business, I couldn't understand why Javier hadn't hired a waitress. Maybe I'd take out a help-wanted ad in the paper tomorrow. I had never been in the restaurant business. There was no way I could run this place alone.

ACKNOWLEDGMENTS

JULIA ALVAREZ: "Snow," copyright © by Julia Alvarez, 1984, 1991, from *How the Garcia Girls Lost Their Accents* (Algonquin Books of Chapel Hill). First appeared in slightly different version in *Warnings: An Anthology of the Nuclear Peril* (Northwest Books, 1984). Reprinted by permission of Susan Bergholz Literary Services, New York, N.Y.

KRISTIN ANDRYCHUK: "Mandy Shupe" first appeared in *The New Quarterly*, Fall, copyright © 1990. Reprinted by permission of the author.

MARGARET ATWOOD: "Bread" first appeared in *Iowa Review*, Vol. 12, No. 2&3, copyright © 1981. Reprinted by permission of the author.

WILL BAKER: "Grace Period," from *Great Stream Review*, Vol. 1, No. 1, copyright © 1989. Reprinted by permission of the author.

SHEILA BARRY: "Corners," copyright © 1992 by Sheila T. Barry. Reprinted by permission of the author.

KENNETH BERNARD: "Vines" first appeared in *Iowa Review*, Spring, copyright © 1978. Reprinted by permission of the author.

HEINRICH BÖLL: "The Cage," translated by Leila Vennewitz, from *The Casualty* by Heinrich Böll, published by Farrar, Straus & Giroux, Inc., English translation copyright © 1986 by the estate of Heinrich Böll and Leila Vennewitz. Reprinted by permission of Farrar, Straus & Giroux, Inc.

RICHARD BRAUTIGAN: "Corporal," from *Revenge of the Lawn* by Richard Brautigan, published by Simon & Schuster, Inc., copyright © 1963, 1964, 1965, 1966, 1969, 1970, 1971 by Richard Brautigan. Reprinted by permission of the Helen Brann Agency.

WILLIAM BROHAUGH: "A Moment in the Sun Field" first appeared in *Negative Capability*, Vol. 9, No. 1, copyright © 1989. Reprinted by permission of the author.

MARLENE BUONO: "Offerings" first appeared in *Story*, Spring, copyright © 1991. Reprinted by permission of the author.

GREGORY BURNHAM: "Subtotals" appeared in *Turnstile*, copyright © 1988, and subsequently appeared in *Harper's*, July, copyright © 1989. Reprinted by permission of the author.

FRANÇOIS CAMOIN: "The Sewers of Salt Lake" first appeared in a different form and under no title in *Sundog, The Southeast Review*, Vol. 11, No. 2, copyright © 1991. Reprinted by permission of the author.

RAYMOND CARVER: "The Father," from *Will You Please Be Quiet, Please?* by Raymond Carver, published by McGraw-Hill, copyright © 1978. Reprinted by permission of International Creative Management, Inc.

KELLY CHERRY: "The Parents," from *My Life and Dr. Joyce Brothers*, copyright © 1990 by Kelly Cherry. Originally appeared in *The North American Review*. Reprinted by permission of Algonquin Books of Chapel Hill.

ACKNOWLEDGMENTS

ADRIENNE CLASKY: "From the Floodlands" first appeared in *The Carolina Quarterly*, Vol. 71, No. 2, copyright © 1989. Reprinted by permission of the author.

BERNARD COOPER: "The Hurricane Ride" first appeared in *Shenandoah*, Vol. 36, No. 4, copyright © 1986. Reprinted by permission of the author.

JULIO CORTÁZAR: "A Continuity of Parks," from *End of the Game and Other Stories*, published by Pantheon, translated by Paul Blackburn, copyright © 1967 by Random House, Inc. Reprinted by permission of Pantheon Books, a division of Random House, Inc.

MICHAEL DELP: "Draft Horse" first appeared in *North Dakota Quarterly*, Vol. 5, No. 4, copyright © 1988. Reprinted by permission of the author.

MARY DILWORTH: "The Factory," from *The Mill*, Millennium Books, copyright © 1986. Originally appeared in *Westerly*. Reprinted by permission of the author.

STUART DYBEK: "Gold Coast," from *The Coast of Chicago* by Stuart Dybek, copyright © 1990 by Stuart Dybek. Reprinted by permission of Alfred A. Knopf, Inc.

BRUCE EASON: "The Appalachian Trail," from *Black Tulips* (Winnipeg: Turnstone Press), copyright © 1991. Originally appeared in *The Fiddlehead*. Reprinted by permission of the Turnstone Press.

CAROL EDELSTEIN: "232-9979," copyright © 1992 by Carol Edelstein. Reprinted by permission of the author.

RUSSELL EDSON: "Dinner Time," from *The Very Thing That Happens* by Russell Edson, published by New Directions, copyright © 1964. Reprinted by permission of the author.

LARRY FONDATION: "Deportation at Breakfast," from *Unscheduled Departures: The Asylum Anthology of Short Fiction*, edited by Greg Boyd, published by Asylum Arts, copyright © 1991. Reprinted by permission of the author.

CAROLYN FORCHÉ: "The Colonel," from *The Country Between Us* by Carolyn Forché, copyright © 1981 by Carolyn Forché. Originally appeared in

Women's International Resource Exchange. Reprinted by permission of HarperCollins Publishers.

K. C. FREDERICK: "Teddy's Canary" first appeared in *Other Voices,* Fall, copyright © 1989. Reprinted by permission of the author.

LARRY FRENCH: "Mr. Mumsford" first appeared in *Mississippi Review,* copyright © 1982. Reprinted by permission of the author.

S. FRIEDMAN: "Here," copyright © 1992 by S. Friedman. Reprinted by permission of the author.

GARY GILDNER: "Fingers," from *The Runner,* published by the University of Pittsburgh Press, copyright © 1978. Reprinted by permission of the author.

ALLAN GURGANUS: "A Public Denial" first appeared in *The Available Press/PEN Short Story Collection* published by Ballantine Books, copyright © 1985 by the PEN American Center. Reprinted by permission of the author.

MARK HALLIDAY: "108 John Street" first appeared in *Denver Quarterly,* Winter, copyright © 1991. Reprinted by permission of the author.

TOM HAWKINS: "Wedding Night" from *Paper Crown* by Tom Hawkins, Book Mark Press, copyright © 1989. Originally appeared in *Ploughshares.* Reprinted by permission of the author.

WILLIAM HEYEN: "Roseville" first appeared in *The Ontario Review,* #27. Reprinted by permission of Time Being Books. Copyright © 1991 by Timeless Press, Inc.

JIM HEYNEN: "What Happened during the Ice Storm," from *You Know What Is Right,* North Point, copyright © 1985. Originally appeared in *Seattle Review.* Reprinted by permission of the author.

SPENCER HOLST: "Brilliant Silence," from *Prose for Dancing,* Station Hill Press, copyright © 1983. Reprinted by permission of the author.

ELLEN HUNNICUTT: "Blackberries" first appeared in *The North American Review,* March, copyright © 1987. Reprinted by permission of the author.

ROD KESSLER: "How to Touch a Bleeding Dog," from *Off in Zimbabwe* by Rod Kessler, University of Missouri Press, copyright © 1985. Originally appeared in *Mazagine*. Reprinted by permission of the author.

JAMAICA KINCAID: "Girl," from *At the Bottom of the River* by Jamaica Kincaid, Farrar, Straus, & Giroux, copyright © 1978, 1983 by Jamaica Kincaid. Reprinted by permission of Farrar, Straus & Giroux, Inc.

FRED LEEBRON: "Water," copyright © 1992 by Fred Leebron. Reprinted by permission of the author.

GORDON LISH: "Fear: Four Examples," from *What I Know So Far* by Gordon Lish, published by Holt, Rinehart, and Winston, and by Scribner and Son, copyright © 1984, 1985. Reprinted by permission of the author.

PAUL LISICKY: "Snapshot, Harvey Cedars: 1948" first appeared in *The Madison Review*, Vol. 11, No. 1, copyright © 1989. Reprinted by permission of the author.

ROBERT HILL LONG: "The Restraints" first appeared in *Quarterly West*, #33, copyright © 1991. Reprinted by permission of the author.

BRET LOTT: "Night," from *A Dream of Old Leaves* by Bret Lott, copyright © 1986, 1987, 1989 by Bret Lott. Reprinted by permission of Viking Penguin, a division of Penguin Books USA, Inc.

MICHAEL MARTONE: "Dish Night" first appeared in *Indiana Review*, Vol. 10, No. 1&2, copyright © 1987. Reprinted by permission of the author.

KATE MCCORKLE: "The Last Parakeet" first appeared in *Alaska Quarterly*, copyright © 1989. Reprinted by permission of the author.

STEVEN MOLEN: "Jane," copyright © 1992 by Steven Molen. Reprinted by permission of the author.

MARY MORRIS: "The Haircut" first appeared in *Special Report*, Aug.–Oct., copyright © 1990. Reprinted by permission of the author.

JOYCE CAROL OATES: "August Evening," copyright © 1988 by The Ontario Review, Inc. From *The Assignation* by Joyce Carol Oates, first published by The Ecco Press in 1988. Reprinted by permission.

DAN O'BRIEN: "Crossing Spider Creek" first appeared in *Texas Review*, Vol. 9, No. 122, copyright © 1988. Reprinted by permission of the author.

TIM O'BRIEN: "Stockings," from *The Things They Carried* by Tim O'Brien, copyright © 1990 by Tim O'Brien. Reprinted by permission of Houghton Mifflin Company/Seymour Lawrence. All rights reserved.

MICHAEL OPPENHEIMER: "The Paring Knife" first appeared in *Sundog*, Vol. 4, No. 1, copyright © 1982. Reprinted by permission of the author.

LON OTTO: "Love Poems," from *A Nest of Hooks* by Lon Otto, copyright © 1978. Reprinted by permission of the University of Iowa Press.

PAMELA PAINTER: "I Get Smart," from *The Company of Cats*, edited by Michael J. Rosen, Doubleday & Company, copyright © 1991. Originally appeared in *The North American Review*. Reprinted by permission of the author.

PAVAO PAVLICIĆ: "A Chronicler's Sin," translated by Miroslav Beker, first appeared in *Special Report*, Aug.–Oct., copyright © 1990. Reprinted by permission of the author.

FRANCINE PROSE: "Pumpkins" first appeared in *Western Humanities Review*, Autumn, copyright © 1989. Reprinted by permission of the author.

BRUCE HOLLAND ROGERS: "The Burlington Northern, Southbound" first appeared in *New Mexico Humanities Review*, 32, copyright © 1989. Reprinted by permission of the author.

CHUCK ROSENTHAL: "The Nicest Kid in the Universe," excerpted from *Experiences with Life and Deaf* by Chuck Rosenthal, Grove-Weidenfeld, copyright © 1985. Originally appeared in *Quarterly West*. Reprinted by permission of the author.

SCOTT RUSSELL SANDERS: "The Philosophical Cobbler," from *Wilderness Plots* by Scott Russell Sanders, William Morrow and Company, copyright © 1983; Ohio University Press, copyright © 1989. Reprinted by permission of the author.

ACKNOWLEDGMENTS

JO SAPP: "Nadine at 35: A Synopsis" first appeared in *The North American Review*, September, copyright © 1981. Reprinted by permission of the author.

DON SHEA: "True Love" first appeared in *Kansas Quarterly*, Vol. 22, No. 3, copyright © 1990. Reprinted by permission of the author.

RICHARD SHELTON: "The Stones," from *You Can't Have Everything* by Richard Shelton, copyright © 1957 by Richard Shelton. First appeared in *Montana Review*. Reprinted by permission of University of Pittsburgh Press.

MARK STRAND: "Space," from *Mr. and Mrs. Baby and Other Stories* by Mark Strand, Alfred A. Knopf, Inc., copyright © 1985. Reprinted by permission of the author.

KENT THOMPSON: "Ponderosa," from *Leaping Up Sliding Away* by Kent Thompson, copyright © 1986 by Kent Thompson. Reprinted by permission of Fiddlehead Poetry Books and Goose Lane Editions.

ROLAND TOPOR: "Feeding the Hungry," translated by Margaret Crosland and David LeVay, from *Stories and Drawings*. Reprinted by permission of Peter Owen, Ltd., London.

JOHN UPDIKE: "The Widow," from *Hugging the Shore* by John Updike. Copyright © 1983 by John Updike. Reprinted by permission of Alfred A. Knopf, Inc.

LUISA VALENZUELA: "Vision Out of the Corner of One Eye," from *Strange Things Happen Here* by Luisa Valenzuela, translation copyright © 1979 by Harcourt Brace Jovanovich, Inc., reprinted by permission of the publisher.

DAVID FOSTER WALLACE: "Everything Is Green" appeared originally in *Puerto del Sol* and *Harper's* and here is reprinted from *Girl with Curious Hair* by David Foster Wallace, with the permission of W. W. Norton & Company, Inc. Copyright © 1989 by David Foster Wallace.

RONALD WALLACE: "Yogurt" first appeared in *Crosscurrents*, Vol. 9, No. 2, copyright © 1990. Reprinted by permission of the author.

ACKNOWLEDGMENTS

DIANE WILLIAMS: "Here's Another Ending," from *This is about the Body, the Mind, the Soul, the World, Time & Fate* by Diane Williams, copyright © 1989. Reprinted by permission of Grove Press, Inc.

LEX WILLIFORD: "Pendergast's Daughter" first appeared in *Quarterly West*, #28, copyright © 1989. Reprinted by permission of the author.

ALLEN WOODMAN: "The Lampshade Vendor," from *The Shoebox of Desire and Other Tales*, published by Swallow's Tale Press, copyright © 1987. Reprinted by permission of the author.

JOANNA H. WOŚ: "The One Sitting There" first appeared in *Malahat Review*, #86, copyright © 1989. Reprinted by permission of the author.